The
SECRET
SISTERS

The
SECRET
SISTERS

AVI

CLARION BOOKS

An Imprint of HarperCollins Publishers

Clarion Books is an imprint of HarperCollins Publishers

Library of Congress Cataloging-in-Publication Data
Names: Avi, 1937– author.
Title: Secret sisters / Avi.
Description: First edition. | New York : Clarion Books, [2023] |
Audience: Ages 8–12. | Audience: Grades 4–6. |
Summary: In the fall of 1925, fourteen-year-old Ida enters a
small-town high school after years of attending a rural one-room
schoolhouse, but the enthusiasm she and her new friends have for
the modern world and modern ways pits them against the school's
old-fashioned principal.
Identifiers: LCCN 2022029565 | ISBN 9780358248088 (hardcover)
Subjects: CYAC: High schools—Fiction. | Schools—Fiction. |
City and town life—Fiction.
Classification: LCC PZ7.A953 Sed 2023 | DDC [Fic]—dc23
LC record available at https://lccn.loc.gov/2022029565

23 24 25 26 27 LBC 5 4 3 2 1

First Edition

This book is for
Lena Frank,
who told me,
"Ida has to go to high school!"

The
SECRET
SISTERS

ONE

AS FAR AS Ida Bidson was concerned, it was the most exciting day in her fourteen years of life: she was about to leave for high school.

It was September 13, 1925, a bright and chilly Sunday morning, when she stepped out of her log cabin home, high among Colorado's Elkhead Mountains. Her sun-rosy face, with hazel eyes and a snub nose, had been scrubbed tingling clean with cold water.

She was wearing a long gray dress her mother had made and a tan cloth coat (store-bought) with an added sheep-wool collar. On her feet were ankle-high, scuffed work shoes. Her long brown hair was braided, the two strands tied off with faded blue ribbons. Ma had fastened them with great care. In Ida's hand was Pa's battered cardboard suitcase. A knotted length of rope kept it closed.

The night before, Ida had said farewell to the chickens and to Snooker, their old horse; patted a few sheep heads (her family ran a sheep ranch); rubbed the ears of Teddy, their sheepdog; and scratched the rump of Bluebell, their milk cow. Since it had been Ida's chore to do the daily milking and feeding, she thought of Bluebell as her cow.

Now, as much as she loved them, she couldn't wait to say goodbye to her human family.

She nuzzled baby Shelby. "Be good," she told him, and when she kissed his fat cheeks he smiled at her, a wet bubble on his pouty pink lips. Next, she gave a rough hair rumple to her seven-year-old brother, Felix. "Don't let Pa and Ma do all my chores," she told him.

"I won't," he promised.

"Be extra nice to Bluebell."

"I will."

"Say hello to everyone at school."

"We have a new teacher."

"Tough on you," Ida said with a grin.

Finally, Ma and Ida hugged.

"I'm going to miss you a lot," Ma whispered into her ear.

"I'll write," Ida said with a smile so wide her face hurt. "And I'll be home for the midterm holiday in November."

"I hope so," said Ma. "Winter is coming, and the car has no side windows. It's a long drive." Reluctant to let her daughter go, she gave Ida another hug. "It's a huge thing you're doing, going away to school. Just be yourself, love. You'll do fine."

"I will. I promise."

Pa was already in their Model T Ford, its motor growling steadily after a couple of backfires. Now he squeezed the rubber bulb on the horn attached to the outside of the car. It sounded like a honking goose with a sore throat. "Need to get a move on, Ida," he called. "You're expected."

Ida put the old suitcase behind the seat and climbed in next to Pa. As soon as she pulled the door shut, Felix dashed forward and stood by the side. "Goodbye, goodbye, goodbye," he chanted.

As Ida laughed, Pa worked the Ford's multiple clutch peddles, adjusted the throttle, and released the brake. When the car lurched forward, Ida bent around, took one last look back at Ma, and waved.

"Goodbye, goodbye, goodbye," Felix called as he ran alongside the car, which was bouncing down the driveway. Falling behind, he stopped and yelled, "Goodbye, goodbye, goodbyyyyye!"

As the car swung onto the dirt road that led into the valley, Ida looked through the cracked windshield at the mountaintops that walled in her world. The summit of Sand Mountain was already sparkling with snow. On the other side, Hahns Peak loomed high. By the road, spruce, lodgepole pine, and aspen trees—the aspen with some early golden leaves—were lined up as if to salute her. About a mile from home, they went by seven battered mailboxes used by local families. It was like crossing a border.

Ida took a deep breath. "At last!" she said. "I'm going to Steamboat Springs." It came out as pure joy. But then, since her last day at her one-room school back in May, it felt like it had taken forever for summer to pass.

Not wanting to wait a moment more, and though she knew the answer, she asked, "How long will it take to get there?"

"Steamboat?" said Pa. "Same as always."

"It's too long," Ida complained cheerfully, wishing she were closer.

Pa said, "Be glad it's not snowing."

As they went along the twisty road, now and again Ida saw a house and pictured the people who lived in it. "I feel sorry for everybody who has to stay up here," she said.

"Oh, I'm guessing we'll manage okay," Pa said lightly.

Five miles on, they passed the one-room schoolhouse where Ida had been a student for seven years and then, for the final six weeks of her last term, the secret teacher. Though that was four months ago, she felt wistful. "I loved being a teacher," she said.

"Hard, though," Pa reminded her.

"Made me want to be a real teacher."

"Worth it, then."

"They've hired a new teacher," Ida informed Pa. "She's only nineteen. From Wyoming. Guess what?"

"What?"

"They have a lady governor in Wyoming. The first in America."

"You going to do that for Colorado?"

"Teacher first," Ida said with a big smile.

"Good plan," said Pa. But after a few silent moments, he said, "There *is* something you need to know. We love you wanting to be a teacher. And you sure showed you could do it. But you wouldn't be going to high school without Miss Sedgewick having invited you to board with her in town."

Miss Sedgewick was the Routt County inspector of one-room schoolhouses who had discovered Ida's secret school and let the students continue so they could take their year-end exams. Impressed with Ida, she had offered a place in her house— for free—so Ida could attend high school in Steamboat.

"Steamboat is the nearest high school you could go to," continued Pa. "But your ma checked; these days room and board in town runs from six to fourteen dollars a week. I don't think we could have managed that. Thought we'd do better this year. But farms and ranches up here are not doing well."

"I thought we were okay," Ida said.

"Were, at first. But farm prices have slid everywhere. The other thing, love, is the jobs you do, the cow, chickens, helping with the sheep, and all the rest. We'll miss you doing that. Worth it if you do well, though. So, your new chores are to get on with Miss Sedgewick and earn good grades."

"I know," said Ida. "And high school is going to be harder than my old school. Like taking Latin. Why do I need that?"

"No idea."

"I don't even know where Latin is," Ida said. "In that letter Miss Sedgewick wrote me, she said I'll have to take five *different* classes. Including some kind of mathematics called algebra. Miss Fletcher was good at teaching all our subjects, but she never taught much math. And in Steamboat, each class has a different teacher. That'll be new."

"You're a quick study, love. Won't take you long to start finding out how smart you are. All I'm saying," said Pa, "is if you want to stay in school, make sure you do well. And doing well won't have anything to do with luck. You've heard me say it often enough: work, not wishes, whips the job. So, work hard."

"I will. Promise."

"Costs lots to run a school," Pa continued. "They need to know you're a good student so they'll continue to welcome you. Sorry to say it, but this may be your best chance."

"Chance for what?"

"Everything."

"What if I can't do it?"

"You'll be milking Bluebell till you're eighty."

Ida laughed. "Then I'll study till my brains turn purple."

"Purple sounds right."

"Pa, what's the best thing about high school?"

"Don't know. Never went."

"How come?"

"Back in Nebraska, where I grew up, we didn't have much schooling nearby."

"You sorry you couldn't go?"

"Didn't have a choice. But I've tried to mind what my father always told me: 'Use what you have, or you'll wind up having nothing.'"

"Pa, I'm only fourteen."

"Guess what's the fastest-moving thing in the world."

"What?"

"Time."

Ida was quiet as they continued to bounce along the rough road. Then she said, "Sometimes Steamboat seems far away."

"Twenty miles. If you had to, you could walk

8

it. And you've visited often enough."

"Routt County is pretty big, though," said Ida. "Did you know it was named after John Long Routt, who was governor of Colorado? Twice. *And* the mayor of Denver. And guess what? Routt County is bigger than the whole state of Rhode Island! Learned all that when we studied Colorado."

"Always love it when you share your facts," said Pa with a smile.

"How big is Steamboat Springs?"

"About thirteen hundred people."

"How many live in Elk Valley?" Elk Valley, where they lived, wasn't a proper town but rather a spread-out township.

"Not certain," said Pa. "These days, maybe fifty."

"It'll be strange living where I don't know *anyone*," Ida said.

"You know Miss Sedgewick. You and your ma visited her home, where you'll be staying."

"But I don't know her very well. Why do you think she isn't married?"

"No idea. But she sure has taken a shine to you. Shouldn't be hard to get along with her."

"Wish Tom was going to school in Steamboat."

Tom was Ida's best friend from the one-room schoolhouse they had attended together.

"What made him decide not to?"

"He found a high school in Denver where they're willing to teach him all about that radio while he has regular classes."

"Nice for him. I'm guessing radio is going to be big."

"Think we'll ever get one?"

"One of these days. Not sure we could get a signal up here yet. Hopefully, we'll have electricity soon. Then a telephone."

"Will Felix be able to do all my chores?"

"He's getting bigger and stronger every day. He's a hard worker. Just do your job, we'll do ours."

After a long silence, Ida said, "Sometimes I kind of feel bad about going off and leaving everyone."

"Ida, love, as I've said, your ma and I never had the chance to get much schooling. Things are different from the time we were your age. Everything is modern. Old ways won't work. You even need high school these days."

"It won't be just high school," said Ida. "To be a real teacher I'll have to go on to a teachers' college. And it's further away. In Greeley."

"You'll get there. Denver," added Pa, "where Tom is going, is about two hundred miles from here."

Ida said, "In cities, teachers can make almost nine hundred dollars a year."

"Probably twice what your teacher here made."

Ida studied the road for a while. "Pa?"

"What's that?"

"You think I'll get any taller?"

"How tall are you now?" Pa replied.

"Almost five feet."

"Oh, sure. Bet you anything you'll be taller than your ma."

Ida, trying to imagine that, smiled.

As they drew closer to town, Ida thought about how more than anything she wanted to go to high school. *Didn't I work fiercely to get here?* she told herself.

"Pa."

"What's that?"

"When I get back home, I want everything to be exactly the same as when I left. Don't let anything change. It's perfect."

Pa laughed. "That's easy."

He swung the car onto Lincoln Avenue, Steamboat Springs' main street.

They passed Fick's Blacksmithing, Steamboat Mercantile, Bank of Steamboat, Light's Clothing Store, Chamberlain's Pharmacy, and other businesses. Ida had seen all these places before when visiting town, but now that she was going to be living here, everything seemed bigger, more imposing.

And in one glance, Ida saw ten or fifteen people on the sidewalks, more folks than she saw in an entire year back home. Most of the women, she noticed, had bobbed hair. She pulled one of her long braids around and studied the blue ribbon. *Are braids going to be okay?* It wasn't something she had considered before. *My ribbons are faded.*

"Ninth Street," said Pa, and he swung the car around the corner only to turn again and come to a stop. "Here's 708 Oak Street," he announced. "Miss Sedgewick's house. Time to start your different life."

Ida took a deep breath. Knowing that her life would not just be different but *new* was exciting.

Pa pulled a large coin from his pocket and offered it to her. "Here, love, save it for something important." It was a Peace Dollar, minted to celebrate the end of the Great War. As far as Ida was concerned, it was a lot of money.

"Thank you," she whispered, and stared at the image of the eagle on the coin. The bird appeared to be a fledgling about to fly for the first time.

Like me, thought Ida, and allowed herself another big grin.

Two

It was Ma and Pa who had built the slightly lopsided log cabin that had always been Ida's home. Even its windows were odd-shaped, because when they were constructing the house, Ma had found cheap used frames at the lumber-yard in town.

Miss Sedgewick's house could not have been more different: a perfectly square two-story building with white clapboard siding, a covered porch (with a couple of wicker chairs), and a sharply angled roof, plus a slender stone chimney. Two windows, with painted blue frames, were on each floor. Under the high front gable was a small triangular window with blue glass.

On the hard dirt street before the house was a parked car, a Chevrolet coupe, a lot newer than the Bidsons' Model T.

"Miss Sedgewick is rich, isn't she?" said Ida.

"You'll find out soon enough." Pa untied the cord that held his door shut and shoved it open. As he and Ida got out of the car, Miss Sedgewick emerged from her front door and stepped to the edge of the porch.

She was a tall woman whose black hair was bobbed. She wore a simple blue drop-waisted dress that reached beneath her knees, and T-strap shoes—with modest heels—were on her feet. Her face was pale but, as far as Ida could tell, friendly.

At the sight of Ida and Mr. Bidson, she smiled, gave a little wave, and called out, "Welcome to your new home!"

Pa put a hand to Ida's back to gentle her forward. "Glad to be here," he returned.

An eager Ida managed to say, "Good afternoon."

"It *is* a good afternoon," said Miss Sedgewick brightly. "Ida, I am *so* glad you've finally arrived. Do come in."

Pa reached around and plucked Ida's suitcase

out of the car, then set it down when he and Ida stepped onto the porch.

"There you go, love." Turning to Miss Sedgewick, he said, "Not to be rude, but I'd best be going. It's a long drive and my sheep are probably bleating for me."

"I understand," said Miss Sedgewick, beaming.

"The missus and I sure do appreciate all you're doing for Ida. Thanks again."

"So happy she's here. I promise to look after her as best I can."

Ida, suddenly wishing that Pa were not leaving quite so fast, gave him a tight hug.

Returning the embrace, Pa leaned over her. "You mind your manners, sweetheart, and learn yourself a whole lot. Work hard and write a note when you have time. Always know we love you." He backed away.

Ida—feeling an unexpected twinge of abandonment—watched him crank the car motor, get into the seat, tie the door shut, give her a last loving look, wave, and then drive off.

For a moment she stood gazing after him, thinking, *I'm on my own*, and couldn't decide if she felt giddy or queasy.

"Would you like to come in, Miss Ida?" Miss Sedgewick asked gently. She was holding the door open.

Ida picked up her suitcase. "Thank you," she said, walking into the front room and looking about. Miss Sedgewick's tidy house was so different from the lived-in clutter she knew at home. She could hardly believe she would be living in such luxury.

But here she was.

It was a spacious, spotless room, the ceiling white, the walls light blue. Two electric light fixtures stuck out from the wall near two framed pictures of flowers. The floor was covered by a dark red rug. There was a couch and, next to it, a standing lamp. A small fireplace. Two chairs before a low table. On the table lay a magazine, the *Saturday Evening Post*. The cover had an illustration of a boy walking toward a school. He didn't look happy.

I'm happy, Ida told herself.

Against one wall stood a cabinet with a glass door, filled with books whose titles meant nothing to Ida. All she recognized was a dictionary, an atlas, and a Sears and Roebuck catalog.

Books, she told herself. *I guess modern people read a lot.*

On top of the cabinet stood a candlestick telephone and a few china figures. On one wall was a photograph of a young man in a military uniform. He had a winsome grin. Ida wondered who he was.

Miss Sedgewick paused before the photo. "That's Ralph Warren. He and I were to be married." Her face slipped into sadness. "But that," she said with a strained smile, "was then. This is now, isn't it? I guess it's always best to be content with what you have."

"My pa," said Ida, "was just telling me what his father always said: 'Use what you have, or you'll wind up having nothing.'"

"Well . . ." said Miss Sedgewick—it came out like a sigh. "Let's bring your suitcase up to your room."

I shouldn't have said that, Ida chided herself.

Miss Sedgewick led her into a small hallway with a staircase. She paused and pointed down the corridor. "I have indoor plumbing. The bathroom is there. The kitchen is here. Do you have a telephone at home?"

"Not yet."

"There's always the post. I know you have that. Just two cents a letter. But my telephone number is one-four-five in case you need it."

"I've never used a telephone."

"Oh my, I must give you a lesson. Can I help you with your suitcase?"

"I'm fine." Clutching the light case with one hand, the banister with the other, Ida followed Miss Sedgewick up to the second story. There was another hallway with three doors. A blue rug was on the floor.

"My bedroom," said Miss Sedgewick, indicating a door. "A little guest room down there. And here's your room." She opened a white door opposite her own.

Ida stepped into the room. Back home, she shared a large, always messy, sleeping loft with her brother. Here, the orderly space was taken up mostly by a single bed, placed against the wall and perfectly made, covered by a multicolored quilt. The bed's iron frame had been painted white. Two pale cotton towels hung over the metal footboard. A chair was also there. The sole sash window had a brown shade with a bottom fringe. In one corner of the room stood a little table upon which sat a metal washbasin that held a glass pitcher of water. Over the table was a small, framed mirror. An electric bulb on a black wire dangled from the ceiling.

It's so neat, thought Ida.

Miss Sedgewick, smiling, pointed. "A closet for all your clothing. I hope there's enough room. Is there anything else I can tell or show you?"

"It's very nice," said Ida, eager to like everything.

"Do you have electricity at home?" asked Miss Sedgewick.

Ida shook her head.

"You'll love it. The light switch is right here." Miss Sedgewick turned it on and off. The light bulb flickered. At Ida's home, they still used candles and kerosene lamps at night.

Ida reached forward and used the switch, something she'd never done before. The burst of light seemed magical.

"Have you had lunch?"

"Yes, thank you," said Ida, who hadn't, but she was too distracted to think of food. She was having two thoughts. *This is so different.* And: *I must get on well with Miss Sedgewick.*

"Now, I've planned for dinner at five. Would

you like to rest, or would you enjoy a stroll over to see the high school?"

"The high school, thank you."

"I'll give you time to unpack first. Shall we go in an hour? Call me if you need anything."

"Thank you, Miss Sedgewick."

"Do call me Gertrude. Or, as my friends do, Trudy."

Trudy reached for the door, then paused and turned back around. For a moment, Ida thought she was going to hug her, but thankfully (for Ida) she held back. But Trudy did say—a small quiver in her voice—"Ida, I'm so happy you're here. It's very special for me."

"Miss Sedgewick . . ."

"Trudy . . ."

"I shouldn't have told you what my grandfather said. That wasn't nice."

"Well," said Trudy with a forced smile, "perhaps it's not always wise to speak everything that's in your mind. But I'll be happy to guide you."

"Guide me?"

"Though Steamboat Springs may be small, as people say, small towns have large eyes and big ears. So, I suppose, being the adult, I may—only

21

if I need to—remind you about . . . oh, the . . . different ways we do things here."

Her words took Ida by surprise. "Different ways?" she asked.

"You know, what's considered proper. Up north, where you live, it may be acceptable to . . . but . . . well, down here, caution and sincerity are best for young ladies."

"I'm . . . I'm just a girl."

"Now, Ida," Trudy said gently, "you *are* starting high school. If that's not becoming a young lady, I don't know what is."

Ida, her eagerness checked, didn't know what to say, and Trudy, with another smile, left the room, shutting the door with a click.

Alone, Ida stood in place, the idea that "small towns have large eyes and big ears" echoing in her head. It sounded like a warning. As did "young lady." *Am I really a young lady?*

Squeezing her hands together, Ida gazed around the room. Now it was Miss Sedgewick's words, "Welcome to your new home, dear," that came to her.

This is not my home, Ida thought. *I'm only staying here.* Then she told herself, *Stop fussing. Everything is fine. Miss Sedgewick is being nice. I must, must do things right.*

She considered the room again. This time it felt smaller, more solitary. At bedtime, in their shared loft, she and Felix always talked, chattering about everything and nothing.

"Just have to talk to myself," Ida mused aloud.

And that bedroom back home had a rough plank ceiling with countless swirls and twists in its grain, so she could imagine anything. Here, the ceiling was smooth and bare. Proper.

"I'll invent smooth fancies," Ida said.

She tried the light switch again. On. Off. On. Off. It *was* amazing.

Even so, she felt anxious. The phrase "small towns have large eyes and big ears" returned. *Miss Sedgewick was telling me there are things I can't do. But I don't know what they are.*

Now, like an unexpected avalanche, worries tumbled through her mind:

To stay in school, I need to do well in my classes.

I need to make Ma and Pa glad I'm going to high school.

I need to make friends.

What if no one likes me?

23

What if I don't like anyone?

Will Miss Sedgewick be nice? What if she's not? Pa's right. I have to get along with her.

The next moment, she recalled her ma's words: "Just be yourself."

Uneasy, Ida sat on the edge of the bed. *Stop it!* she scolded herself again. *This is what I wanted to do. I'm lucky to be here. Miss Sedgewick—Trudy—is being kind. I need to be thankful. And thoughtful. I want to be a teacher, which means I have to go to high school and do well. I have to be a young lady. I have to act properly.*

Wanting to regain her earlier excitement, Ida hung up her coat, opened her suitcase, and set her three dresses—made by her mother—in the closet. They didn't take up much space.

It was only when she took out her flannel nightgown that she saw a note at the bottom of the suitcase written in her mother's hand: *We love you!* Below were three signatures: *Ma, Pa, Felix.*

Ida's eyes welled. *Young ladies don't cry,* she told herself sternly even as she smeared a tear away.

With care, Ida put her folded socks and cotton underclothing on the small closet shelf. She placed a pair of slender new shoes on the floor. She slid

Pa's suitcase—with the rope inside—under the bed. Her amber hairbrush and comb (last year's Christmas present from Ma and Pa) were set on the little table.

Ida noticed a small gap in the mirror frame and tucked the dollar coin Pa had given her into it so she would always see the gift. She could not imagine ever spending it.

Next to the coin, she slipped in her family's *We love you!* note.

Unpacking done, Ida sat on the edge of the bed again. Trudy had said they would walk to the school in an hour. That felt like a long time away. At home, there was always something to be done. She thought of Ma and missed her. Felix, too. Pa. Shelby. Teddy the dog. Bluebell the cow.

I mustn't get homesick. No, never be homesick.

She went to the mirror. Her hazel eyes, she decided, were the same color as Bluebell's. She wanted to smile but couldn't.

Ida stared at herself. "You're here to work," she said. "Just do what's right, and it'll all be good."

She had been cheerful this morning, almost dizzy. Now she was fretful. And tomorrow she would start school.

That made her remember something Tom had once told her: "If you want to try something new, and you're not scared, means you're not really trying something new."

Well then, thought Ida, *tomorrow will be the scariest day of my life!*

THREE

Feeling the need to get out of the small room, Ida stepped into the hall. She carefully shut the door behind her and, trying to be quiet, went slowly down the steps, gripping the banister. Not seeing Trudy in the living room, she went on to the kitchen.

Miss Sedgewick was seated at a small, round table, reading a book. A cup and saucer were before her. A magazine—*Good Housekeeping*—lay on the table. On its cover was a picture of a young woman holding a sweet little girl in her arms. *Is she supposed to be a mother?* Ida wondered. She seemed so young.

Ida gazed about the well-ordered, gleaming room. The smooth walls were painted white, the floor covered in checked-pattern linoleum. There was a sink and an open cupboard filled with cans of food. Ida had never seen so many cans in a home. There was also a book, *The Boston Cooking-School Cookbook*, along with some pots and pans. At home, they had a few books but no cookbooks. Ma always knew—beans to bread—what to do. *I'm in the modern world now*, Ida told herself. *I need to learn modern things.*

Higher up were a couple of canisters marked "Flour" and "Sugar." Ida doubted she could even reach them. *I need to grow taller, too!*

Trudy looked up, saw Ida, smiled, and put her book down. "Ah, here you are. This is my new kitchen," she said. "Do you like it? Mr. Dalzell delivers ice for the icebox. I only have to drain the water twice a week. And this is an electric stove."

The stove was enameled white with the name "Fidelity" in black on the oven door. It stood on tall legs and had three burners, plus a side oven. A starched tea towel hung from the oven handle.

Impressed, Ida said, "It's very nice." At Ida's home, cooking was done on their wood-burning iron stove, which stood, big, black, and always warm, in the main room. For cold storage, they had a large stone-lined box set deep in the ground outside.

"Would you like to join me in a cup of tea?"

"No, thank you," said Ida. She had heard of tea but had never drunk any.

For a moment neither spoke.

"Well," Trudy said brightly, "shall we go for that stroll about town? See the high school? It's just a short walk."

Ida nodded and said, "When do I start classes?"

"Tomorrow morning, eight thirty. You'll have a grand time."

Into Ida's head came Pa's voice: "Use what you have, or you'll wind up having nothing."

Then she recalled Trudy's words: "Be content with what you have."

As they headed out the front door, Ida wondered how she could fit those two ideas together.

"There's your high school," Trudy said with a wave of her hand when they reached the corner of Seventh and Pine Streets. "Built just seven years ago," she added with pride. "I had already been teaching a few years when I moved here."

Ida gazed at the building. It seemed gigantic. Three stories high, all brick, with ten windows across the first level and three large windows that covered the higher floors. There were two double-door entrances, one on the right side and one on the left. Before the school lay a wide grass lawn.

As Ida looked at the high school, she couldn't help but think about her one-room school, a small, squat wooden building with walls of peeling white paint and a poky bell steeple, the bell long gone; the front yard was weeds and dirt. As far as Ida knew, the school had been there forever.

Ida asked, "Do a lot of students go here?"

"This year, eighty-seven I think."

Ida's old school had had eight, and that included herself and her brother.

"How many teachers?"

"About fifteen."

Her old school had one teacher.

"Where are the privies?"

"Inside," said Trudy, appearing to suppress a smile. "Complete with plumbing. I have my office here," she went on. "But I'm often gone. My job has me visiting the one-room schoolhouses all over the county. Just like when I visited your school and met you. Tomorrow I need to go south to Toponas. Which means I'll be gone all day."

Ida, still staring at the big building, said, "How will I know which classes I'm taking?"

"Tomorrow is registration day. A shortened day. You'll just walk in and sign up. They'll give you your class schedule, textbooks, and home-room assignment."

"What's homeroom?"

"That's the room where you start each day. For attendance. Announcements. Things like that. Then you go to classes to meet your teach-ers and get textbooks. I promise it'll be simple."

Ida tried to imagine how many rooms the building had and hoped she wouldn't get lost.

She went up to the entry and peered through the glass. What she saw was an empty hallway with several closed doors. At the far end hung three pictures: George Washington, Abraham Lincoln, and someone else. Seeing the two presi-dents was reassuring. She had seen their likenesses in her old school.

"Is that third man the mayor of Steamboat?" she asked.

Trudy looked. "Calvin Coolidge. President of the United States."

Embarrassed, Ida stepped away, thinking, *There's so much I need to learn.*

She followed Trudy back down the walkway toward the street. As they reached it, a car drove up. Unlike Ida's family's car, it was a new Model T Ford, all enclosed.

A man dressed in a white suit, a panama straw hat on his head, stepped out of the driver's seat, then touched a finger to his hat brim by way of greeting Miss Sedgewick and Ida. The next moment, a girl burst out of the passenger side. She was leggy-tall, thin-faced, with bobbed hair, wearing a short, drop-waisted, pleated pink dress and green socks that reached her knees. On her head was a blue cloche hat. There was also a touch of red on her bow-shaped lips.

"There you go, babe," the man said to the girl. "Here's where you start in the morning."

The girl studied the school for a moment, then turned to Ida. "Hey, I'm Lulu," she said. "I'm supposed to begin here tomorrow. Would you believe it? Me, in Steamboat High." She gestured to the man. "My butter-and-egg man. My mother died of the flu. We just moved to town from Craig. Do you go here? Know anything about this killjoy place?"

Ida, simultaneously intrigued and baffled by Lulu's fast talking, could only repeat "Killjoy?"

"Don't mind my daughter, miss," said the man, his voice loud and jovial. "She loves flinging flapper slang. She's asking if you know anything about the school." He laughed heartily. "I'm always translating." With a tip of his hat, he turned to Miss Sedgewick. "How do, ma'am. Quinton Gallagher is my moniker. Insurance my trade. The Be Sure Insurance Company, 212 Lincoln Ave. Newly arrived in town. Greatly gratified to make your acquaintance. Is this your delightful daughter?"

"Thank you," said Trudy, "but no." She touched Ida's shoulder. "This is Ida Bidson. My boarder. She's about to start high school too."

"Jeepers creepers," Lulu said to Ida, "is there anything worse than skipping into a party and being the only oil can? So, don't worry. I'll be your duck's quack, okay? Just know, I'm peppy. Get it?"

"I think so," Ida said. Fascinated by the way the girl was talking, Ida was almost certain Lulu was offering her friendship.

"You're a sweet cookie," Lulu went on. "Would you believe it, babes got the vote, but I talked to someone who goes here and there are no clubs. Not one. Clubs are the cat's pajamas. The best. Do whatever you want. Soon as school starts, I'm going to kick the can and get a club bouncing down the road."

Ida decided: she wanted this girl to be her friend.

"Let's get going, Lulu," said Mr. Gallagher. "Miss Gemelli is waiting at church. You know how she hates to wait."

At the name Miss Gemelli, Lulu showed a sour face to Ida, clearly revealing what she thought of the woman, even as she said, "Just wanted to peep the school. Hey, snail's elbows to meet you, Miss Ida. Let's do some spilling tomorrow."

"Ain't she the flapper lapper?" boomed a grinning Mr. Gallagher with another tip of his hat. "Pleasure to meet you." Father and daughter got into the car. In moments they drove off.

Ida and Trudy stood gazing after them. "My goodness," Trudy exclaimed. "How young people talk these days. Not very ladylike. Did you understand anything that girl was saying? 'Snail's elbows.' I'm sure there are no such things. 'Butter-and-egg man,' I think that's her father. But 'spilling.' What do you guess *that* meant?"

"Don't know. I think she's nervous about starting school."

"Goodness," said Trudy. "I hope she doesn't become your friend. Is that nice boy—Tom, I think was his name—coming to school here too?"

"He went to Denver."

"Did he?"

"To study radio."

"Good for him."

"What is . . . a club?" Ida asked.

"A group of some sort that does things together. I belong to the Steamboat Women's Club. I don't think you'll want to be in that girl's club. Rather common, don't you think?"

Ida shrugged. "I thought she seemed . . . fun."

"But I'm sure you don't want her to be a friend."

I do, Ida thought, but didn't say.

"Shall we head on back home?" Trudy asked.

On the way, they walked down the town's main street, Lincoln Avenue. "That's the pharmacy," Trudy pointed out as they went along. "They have a lovely soda fountain there. That's the bank. That's the brand-new town hall. Isn't it grand? Remind me to take you to the library on Sixth Street. It recently reopened. Mrs. Molly, the librarian, is a special friend. Are you a reader?"

"I like reading, but we don't have many books at home."

"I read a lot," said Trudy. "That building is a feed store. That's the Orpheum, where they show moving pictures. Do you like movies?"

"I've never seen one," said Ida.

"Really! Just thirty cents a ticket. But I'm afraid very few are decent. Full of wild behavior. I'll find a nice one to take you to. It's said they'll have sound soon."

All Ida could think was *There are so many new things here. Hope Miss Sedgewick lets me do some.*

When they returned to the house, Trudy said, "Now, Ida, I hope you consider this your home. Feel free to go about wherever you'd like. No need to ask. If anything is lacking, tell me. And if you find a book in my cabinet you'd enjoy reading, please help yourself. They are all quite acceptable. I'll start dinner."

"Can I help?" Ida asked as they entered the living room.

"Just relax."

After Trudy left the room, Ida sat on the stiff couch, thinking about the high school and that girl, Lulu. *She was interesting. What a name! And her bobbed hair . . . If all the girls in school talk and act like that, I'll have to learn what they mean. Maybe Lulu could teach me.*

Ida fingered her braids.

At home, the nearest neighbors, a mile away, were the Sibleys. They were elderly. Ida had no girlfriends her own age. She would like some. A girls' club might be fun.

Ida flicked open the copy of the *Saturday Evening Post*. The advertisements were for things she didn't recognize.

She put the magazine aside and drifted across the room to look at the books. The titles meant nothing to her. Knowing what an atlas was, she pulled it out, then took it to the porch and sat in one of the wicker chairs. Now and again a car passed, as did a few strolling people. No one paid Ida any mind.

She opened the atlas and hunted for a map of Colorado. When she found one, "Denver" was right there in bold letters. It took some searching to find "Steamboat Springs" printed in little letters.

She looked for Elk Valley. It wasn't there. *I'm from nowhere*, Ida told herself.

She moved on, turning the pages idly and

recognizing a few names: France, Germany, England. She had heard of those places but knew almost nothing about them. And the book had lots of maps showing countries she had never heard of either—like Denmark and Argentina. She searched for the country called Latin but couldn't find it. As she flipped through the book, she felt as if the world were getting bigger.

Trudy called her for dinner.

"A special welcome," she said as she set a plate before Ida.

Ida wondered what she was about to eat: something pale pink on a piece of toast, partly covered with a blob of white. Off to one side, a pile of faded peas.

"That's canned salmon with white sauce," said Trudy. "A new recipe from my most recent *Good Housekeeping* magazine. It does give me joy to cook for someone else. And it's so much easier with canned goods—like that salmon and those peas—don't you think?"

Ida, who had never eaten salmon, nodded and chewed slowly, trying to decide what she thought of it. *Not much taste.*

All through dinner Trudy asked questions about Ida's family, her brother, the sheep, and where her parents came from.

Ida answered—she felt she had to—and finally asked, "Do you have family here?"

"As you can see, I have no children. And my parents have passed away. I do have an older sister—along with her husband and my nieces and nephews—up in Sioux Falls, South Dakota. I'm afraid I don't see them much.

"Now, Ida, speaking of family, you are going to have to help me know when and how I can be most helpful to you. I expect we'll have dinner together every night. Share our day's doings. I'm not your mother, of course, but I suppose I'll need to try and act like one. *In loco parentis.* That's Latin for 'in the place of a parent.'"

Ida, alarmed, thought, *I don't need another parent*, but all she said was "Thank you." She hoped she sounded sincere.

"Here's dessert. My favorite. Baked French custard."

Fortunately, Ida liked it. "Guess what?" she said. "There's a part of France that's an island: Corsica. I saw it in your atlas."

"That's good to know," said Trudy with a smile.

By eight o'clock, a tired Ida lay in her bed,

trying to get used to the soft mattress. In the dark room, random thoughts spun through her head: *Canned salmon. Phooey. Movies. That might be fun. Calvin Coolidge, president. Remember what he looks like. Are we poor? And that girl—Lulu. What a fun name. How fast she talked. A club. The cat's pajamas. Wonder what pajamas are. Bobbed hair. Maybe I should cut my hair. A drop-waisted, pleated pink dress and green socks. Lipstick! French custard.* In loco parentis. *Miss Sedgewick. Trudy. Is she what I'll become when I'm an adult? Everything here is modern, but she seems old-fashioned. How could she not like Lulu just because of the way she talks? I must get along with Trudy. But I want to be modern. Is Lulu modern?*

Ida got out of bed to turn on the electric light. It was too bright. She turned it off. No, she needed to get used to new things. *It'll help me read better.* She turned the light back on and looked across the room toward the mirror. Being able to see her family's note and Pa's Peace Dollar made her feel good. She climbed into bed again, only to get out to turn the light off. *Can't just blow out a candle anymore.*

Pulling the blankets up to her chin, Ida thought about how in the morning she'd be going to that enormous school. Her first day of high school! *Hope I remember the way there. It'll be full of new people. I need to be friendly. Smart. I must do well. I'm too excited to fall asleep!*

But it felt like only seconds had passed when she heard a tap on her door and Trudy's voice saying:

"Ida, dear. Time for school."

FOUR

IDA PUT ON her favorite dress: the blue checked gingham her mother had made for her. Thinking about what Lulu had worn—the drop-waisted, pleated, short dress and high socks—Ida fretted that her long dress might be judged old-fashioned. It was something she had never thought about before.

She wondered if her ma could make up-to-date dresses. Did her mother even know what was up-to-date? Anyway, Ma was back home, twenty miles north.

Stop thinking silly things! Ida berated herself. *No*

reason to be nervous. Everything will be okay. I'm going to high school at last!

In the bathroom downstairs, she washed her face with warm water and brushed her teeth with cold water. She liked having both. That was something else new.

Back in her room, she made her bed, then stood in front of the mirror to fix her hair and wondered if she'd be the only girl with braids. She heard her mother's words: "Just be yourself, love. You'll do fine."

She said it aloud in her mother's voice. It steadied her. She also touched Pa's coin, and then the family note. At the same moment, she remembered Pa's saying: "Work, not wishes, whips the job."

As Ida stood there, she reminded herself that this was the day she had wanted to happen for so long. *I did it. I did it*, she told herself. *I'm going to high school.* She smiled at her mirror image only to decide her pigtails were ugly. The next instant she found herself wishing Felix were going to school with her.

"You look very nice, dear," Trudy said when Ida appeared in the kitchen.

Breakfast consisted of an omelet, toast, and a glass of milk. Also set out was a small pot of honey. Ida, feeling she had grasshoppers in her stomach, decided she was too excited to eat.

"That toast is Wonder Bread," prompted Trudy. "That's how modern we are. Not hungry? Are you all right?"

"Just want everything to get started," Ida admitted.

"It'll be fine," Trudy assured her, patting Ida's hand, which Ida didn't like. *I'm not sure I'm really a young lady*, she thought, *but I'm definitely not a baby.*

"Now, you must tell me what foods you like. Did you enjoy that salmon last night?"

"It was very good," said Ida, feeling obliged to be positive.

"Then I'll be sure to make it again."

"I suppose I can eat most anything," Ida said. "And I can cook. A bit. At home, I help my ma."

"Lovely. Sometimes I get home late, so I'll remember that. Now, do you want me to walk you to school?"

"Thank you," said Ida, inwardly relieved because she wasn't certain she'd be able to remember the way.

They walked in silence, Ida hoping Trudy

couldn't hear her heart pounding. *I'm going to high school*, she told herself. She had to keep from skipping. *Skipping is for little kids.*

They turned onto Pine Street, and Ida saw a crowd of young people—more girls than boys—moving toward the school. She stopped and stared.

Most of the boys were wearing caps and knickers. Some wore overalls and boots. It was surprising to see so many as big as adults. *Are those young men students?*

Ida noticed the way the girls looked and dressed. Like Lulu, most had bobbed hair and colorful drop-waisted dresses, dresses shorter than hers. Only a few wore their hair long. None had braids. *I'm so short*, thought Ida. *They're going to think I'm young.*

Abruptly deciding she didn't want to approach school with someone who might be taken for her mother, she announced, "I think I can find my way now."

"Are you quite sure?" asked Trudy.

"I guess that's where all those kids are going," said Ida.

"Fine. I knew you were fearless. Now, have a peachy day. I'll be at Toponas most of the day."

As Ida moved quickly down the street, Trudy

called, "I never lock the front door. We'll meet up at dinner."

"Thank you," said Ida, nervous and excited to be heading toward the crowd of girls and boys.

Many of the students walked in small groups and seemed to know one another. Among them, there was much laughter and chatter. Ida told herself she should talk to someone but, feeling shy, held back.

Then she realized she'd put on the wrong shoes, her regular ranch ones, high and scuffed. For a moment she considered running back to Miss Sedgewick's house to change, only to tell herself she must not be late. No! And what if she lost her way?

As the students passed into the school, an older man—with a pale, potato-white face, hair parted in the middle, high starched collar, black tie, and perfectly round wire eyeglasses pressed upon his big nose—was greeting many students by name. "Hello, Homer. Welcome back, Polly. Have a good summer, Hiram?"

By his side was a large brown dog—a German shepherd—his tail wagging happily.

A few students patted the dog's head. "Hello, Major," they said.

When the man merely nodded to Ida without speaking, she wondered who he was. *Should I have said something?*

The man was calling out, "New students, turn left and register. Returning students, go to your right."

Ida stepped into the building. *I'm in high school!* She felt as if she were glowing.

At the end of the crowded, chatter-filled hallway, beneath the portraits of the three presidents, there was a T. Most students turned to the right. Ida, among some twenty-five others, went to the left, and then she stopped at the back of a line. She peered around and saw a table, behind which stood a slim woman in a green dress. *Is she a teacher?* To Ida's eyes, she seemed too young to be one.

Ida noticed that the woman's dress had embroidery trimming on the collar, bodice, and sleeves. She was wearing a hat over her bobbed hair. Piles of paper were stacked around her. As each student approached, the woman smiled, chatted a bit, sorted through some papers, then handed the student a sheet.

Ida felt a poke on her shoulder. She turned. A tall girl was standing right behind her. Her bobbed hair was black, her face round with big eyes and a sharp nose. She was biting her lower lip. "Is this where we're supposed to be?" she said.

"This is the registration line for new students," said Ida.

"I'm new," said the girl. "Oh, I'm Becky Floyd."

"I'm Ida Bidson," said Ida, glad to be speaking to someone.

As the line moved forward, Becky said, "I live back on Logan Avenue. Where's your home?"

"North Routt. Elk Valley."

"Creepers. That's a long way, isn't it?"

"I'm boarding."

"People say this is a hard school," Becky said as she looked past Ida toward the table. "My father said if I flunk out, I'll have to find a job or get myself handcuffed."

"Handcuffed?" said Ida, not understanding.

"You know, married. Or at least engaged."

Ida was amazed. The few girls she knew who had married had only done so in their twenties.

"And I don't even like boys," Becky added.

"Next, please!" came a voice.

Ida spun about.

The young woman standing behind the table was looking down at her, the expression on her face friendly. "Welcome to Steamboat High," she said with a smile. "Is this the first time you're here?"

"Yes, please."

"So glad to meet you. I'm the new teacher. My name," said the woman, "is Miss Martha Mickle. The mathematics and music teacher. All *M*s," she added with a big grin. "We can be pals. What grade level are you entering?"

"First year."

"Wonderful. Now please tell me who you are and where you went to grade school."

"Ida Bidson. Elk Valley schoolhouse."

"That's North Routt, isn't it? I hope you're not traveling here every day, are you?"

"I'm boarding."

"Smart girl. A fair number seem to be."

She reached for one of the paper piles and shuffled through it. Not finding what she was searching for, she glanced up, looking concerned. "Oh dear, Miss Bidson. I'm afraid I don't see your certificate of completion here. Did you finish eighth grade?"

Ida, taken aback by the question, said again, "Yes, please."

"Hmm," said the teacher, looking perplexed. "Your certificate isn't here. I'm afraid I can't give you a schedule without it."

Confused, Ida said, "What should I do?"

"You'll need to bring in the form that says you finished eighth grade."

Having known nothing about it, Ida just stood there. She was trembling.

Miss Mickle offered an encouraging smile. "Just go down to the main office. I'm sure they can sort it out."

"Thank you," Ida struggled to say. She turned away only to stop and ask, "Where . . . where's the . . . office?"

"Down the hall and to the right. Ask for Miss Ogden, Mr. Langly's secretary—Mr. Langly is the principal—and explain your situation. She'll be able to help you."

In a state of shock, Ida walked unsteadily back along the hall, wondering what had happened. What if she was not allowed to attend school? Was her high school dream over already?

"Hey, Miss Ida, get your classes?"

Ida stopped and turned. It was the girl—

Lulu—that she had met yesterday.

"Got your classes?" Lulu repeated when Ida didn't respond.

"Uh . . . no," Ida mumbled, still trying desperately to make sense of what was going on.

"I did," said Lulu, waving a paper as she moved on. "Not exactly giggle water. I'm trying to find out if anyone is going to have a party. I love cutting a rug. Hey, babe, is everything nifty? You look like someone slapped an icy mitt cross your face."

Ida didn't understand the words, though she recognized the tone of concern. Grateful for the sympathy but frantic to fix her problem, she muttered, "Thank you . . . but . . . I have to go," and hurried away. Halfway down the entry hall, she found an open door. When she looked in, she saw an office of some kind. No one was there. Not knowing what else to do, she entered and stood before a desk.

Five minutes passed. No one came. Increasingly panicked, Ida spun about, then walked from the office, down the hallway, and out of the building.

Her dread turning into anguish, she stood on the top step of the entryway. She didn't even know where her certificate of completion was, though apparently everyone else had theirs. The other kids were already in class, and she couldn't even register.

I can't go to high school.

She thought of telephoning Miss Sedgewick. Something about a number: 145. Then she realized she didn't know where a telephone was, and besides, she had never used one. What's more, Trudy told her she'd be gone all day.

Feeling sicker than ever, Ida stood in place, fighting—and failing—to hold back tears. Then she remembered that Pa had said home was only twenty miles away. She could walk. If she started now, she'd be home by night. She took one step and then stopped.

"No!" she said aloud in a firm voice. "I want to go to school! I have to! There must be a way!"

With that, she turned and started toward the building.

FIVE

IDA HADN'T EVEN REACHED the school doorway when she saw a car speed down the street and come to a squeaky halt. The next moment Trudy jumped out, waving a piece of paper.

"Ida!" Trudy cried as she hurried to the walkway. "I'm so sorry. I completely forgot to give you this." She held out the paper. "Your certificate of completion. Forgive me. I truly meant to give it to you. Have you been standing here long?"

Ida struggled to say, "It's all right," as she took the paper and glanced at it.

This certifies that <u>Ida Bidson</u>, age <u>14</u>, a resident of the town of <u>Elk Valley</u>, of <u>Routt</u> County, State of Colorado, has completed the course of study <u>with honors</u> prescribed for common schools, and is entitled to enter the high school at <u>Steamboat Springs</u>, for the year beginning <u>September 1925</u>.

Yours truly,
Miss Gertrude Sedgewick
County Examiner

"Just take that inside," said Trudy. "You'll be registered right away. I promise you. There's nothing to be worried about."

Ida, feeling deep relief, managed to say, "Thank you." She forced a smile and hoped there were no tears.

"I'm so *very* sorry," repeated Trudy. "Living alone, I forget how to take care of someone else." She stood there, an embarrassed smile on her face, as if waiting for Ida to forgive her.

"I'll be fine," said Ida, and turned about and went into the school. Once inside, she paused and peeked through the doorway windows. Miss Sedgewick was driving away. Ida wiped the tears off her cheeks.

Taking deep breaths, she walked down the

empty hallways to where that nice teacher had been at the registration table. To Ida's further relief, Miss Mickle was still there, piling up papers. As Ida approached, Miss Mickle smiled warmly. "Oh, good. All sorted out?"

Ida, her hand shaking, offered the certificate paper.

Miss Mickle looked at it. "Perfect. No more than a silly mix-up." She smiled again. "Nothing to fret about. We still going to be pals?"

Ida gave a weak nod and made herself smile.

Miss Mickle pulled out a form and wrote Ida's name at the top, then handed it to her. "Here's your schedule, Ida. All good. You'll see. I'm your math and music teacher."

Ida managed another "Thank you" and looked at the paper.

Ida Bidson
Freshman
Assigned classes:
8:45–9:00. Homeroom. Room 106. Miss Blake.
9:00–9:45. Algebra. Room 219. Miss Mickle.
9:45–10:30. Latin. Room 202. Mr. Roscoe.
10:30–11:15. Study Hall. Room 202.
11:15–Noon. English. Room 212. Miss Castle.

Noon–1:00. Lunch.
1:00–1:45. Study Hall. Room 110.
1:45–2:30. General Science. Room 115.
Mr. Hanson.
2:30–3:15. Music. Room 223. Miss Mickle.
3:15. Dismissal.

"What do I do now?" Ida asked.

"Go on to your homeroom, 106. It's right along there. That'll be Miss Blake." Miss Mickle pointed the way and offered up her smile again. "Just show her your schedule."

"Thank you," Ida muttered, and headed down the deserted hallway, passing classrooms with closed doors and muffled voices within.

Everybody else has started.

Seeing "106" over a doorframe, she stopped, took a deep breath, and whispered, "Okay. Really, really starting."

She stepped into the classroom and shut the door softly behind her. The room was full of students seated at four rows of desks. At the front, a woman—Ida assumed she was the teacher, Miss Blake—was positioned behind a large desk. She was dressed in black and stood very erect. Her dark eyebrows made her seem severe. "Yes?" she said to Ida. "Can I help you?"

The students swiveled around and looked at Ida.

Uncomfortably aware that everyone was watching her, Ida raised her schedule. "I . . . I think I'm supposed to be here."

The teacher held out a hand.

Ida went forward and passed the paper to her. The woman took it, glanced over it, and gave it back. "Correct. I'm Miss Blake, your homeroom teacher. Find a seat. And Miss Bidson, since you're new here, you need to be aware that it's not acceptable to be late. If you are late for class, you'll need a late slip. We'll ignore that this time."

Mortified by both the rebuke and the scrutiny of the other students, Ida searched for a place to hide. At the far back of the room, a redheaded girl was sitting alone. Ida took the empty desk next to her.

Once seated, she placed clasped hands on the desk. Feeling exhausted, she briefly closed her eyes. *I made it.* Then she glanced about the room.

There were twelve students—she counted them—boys and girls. Thankfully, no one was looking at her anymore.

Some of the girls seemed quite old and tall. Some of the boys were young and short. They looked ordinary but, as far as Ida could tell, nice.

Each student had an individual desk with a wooden top attached to a metal frame, the frame bolted to the floor. Every desk had an inkwell. The room's plain walls had no decoration. There was one large window.

Up front, Miss Blake was reciting a list of rules without any emotion. "No chewing gum allowed anywhere in the school. Do not run through the hallways. Not only is smoking bad for you, but it's also not allowed in school. No shouting or screaming. No . . ."

Ida peeked at the redheaded girl sitting at the next desk. She was staring straight ahead. Ida decided the girl was showing disapproval of her. Feeling the need to defend herself, Ida murmured, "My certification paper was mixed up."

The girl dipped her chin but didn't look around.

"I'm new here," Ida added, wanting to explain more.

"Miss Bidson," called Miss Blake from the front of the room. "It's unfortunate enough that you were late. If you are going to get along here, you need to pay attention to our rules. I just said there is *no* talking during class. May I remind you, though you *were* late, you are *now* in class."

Ida, painfully aware that the other students were staring at her again, felt her face become hot, even as she kept her eyes on the teacher. "Yes, ma'am," she stammered.

"Now," continued Miss Blake, "with today's shortened schedule, you will go on to your next class, meet your teacher, and get textbooks, if any. Check your schedule, then go ahead to your other classes. Every day, you'll start off right here, since this is your homeroom, with me. Tomorrow we'll start regular-length classes. Each one is forty-five minutes long. Any questions? No? Dismissed. Enjoy your day."

Enjoy? thought Ida. It was not the word she'd use to describe her first day of high school so far. *What's the next thing that will go wrong?*

SIX

WITH A CLATTER of banging desk seats, the students came to their feet. Ida jumped up too.

"Didn't mean to get you in trouble," said the redheaded girl. "I'm Dorothy Kovács. You can call me Dot." She paused a moment, then added, "From Oak Creek."

"I'm Ida. From North Routt."

Ida contemplated the girl. She was taller than Ida—*everyone was*—and had bobbed hair. Against that frame of red locks, her face was very pale. She was wearing a simple old-fashioned dress, not, Ida was glad to note, drop-waisted.

Welcoming friendly words, Ida asked, "Where's your next class?" She and Dot walked side by side into a crowded hallway.

Dot looked at her schedule. "Algebra, room 219."

"Me, too," said Ida. "Must be upstairs. The steps are over there."

"I'm glad I don't have that Miss Blake for any classes," said Dot. "Seems a splosh."

"Guess so," said Ida. Though she wasn't sure what "splosh" meant, it sounded right. "Where's Oak Creek?"

"About twenty miles south."

"Are you boarding?"

Dot shook her head.

"How do you get here?"

"I worked it out. The train stops near my home and picks me up. I ride in the engineer's cab." The girl smiled shyly. To Ida's eyes, there was something forced about her expression, something strained.

"Just have to be careful about coal dust," Dot went on. "I go back the same way. There's a one thirty. And a five twenty. Otherwise, the next train is at eight thirteen. Here's the steps."

Ida, curious about the girl, followed along. They went up one level and started down another hallway. Ida, checking the numbers over the doors, announced, "Room 219."

The room was no different than their homeroom, save that there was a new teacher. Ida was glad to see that it was Miss Mickle—the "all *Ms*" one—whom she had met when she registered. On the teacher's desk were two piles of books.

Students filed in and found seats, Ida taking a place next to Dot, who again chose the back row. "Is your whole schedule like mine?" Ida asked.

Dot handed over her paper.

Ida looked at it. "Oh, good. It's the same," she said. "We can keep each other from getting lost. I'm so glad to know someone."

"Same for me," said Dot.

"All right, girls and boys, my name is Miss Mickle. Welcome to high school. So glad to see you all. Hello, Miss Ida," the teacher said cheerfully. "All sorted out, I see."

Ida, increasingly relaxed, smiled back.

"Since everyone is new here," said Miss Mickle to the class, "things can be confusing. This is my first year here too. I'm from Wisconsin."

Into Ida's head popped a memory from when she studied geography. She raised her hand.

"Yes, Miss Bidson?"

"Wisconsin's principal product is dairy."

Miss Mickle laughed. "Exactly right. I'm cheesy too. Now, this is freshman algebra." She went on to describe the class and then passed out textbooks to the students. The book was titled *Algebra One*, by Hadley and Swift.

Ida opened her copy. Pasted on the inside cover was a form.

Name   Date Received   Book Condition   Date Returned

There were columns beneath each heading. Under "Name," there was a list of handwritten signatures. The dates went back to 1914. Under "Book Condition," the first listing read *New*. By the last entry, ten years later, the condition of the book was noted as *Old*.

"Write your names on the inside cover," said Miss Mickle. "Along with the rest of the information."

Ida, feeling a jolt of embarrassment, realized she had brought nothing with which to write. *What kind of a high school student am I?* She pressed a hand over her eyes. *I'm just not thinking.*

"Want to borrow my pen?" Dot offered quietly.

Ida nodded thankfully, releasing a breath she hadn't known she'd been holding. While waiting for Dot to finish writing, she flipped through the math book. It was filled with numbers, letters, and a vast array of mysterious signs, none of which she understood. *I'll never learn this.* One page was torn. Scribbles and doodles appeared here and there.

"You know any algebra?" Ida asked as she took Dot's pen. It was a simple wooden one with a metal nib.

Dot shook her head.

Ida dipped the pen into the desk's inkwell and filled in the form with her name and the date. Under "Book Condition," she wrote, *Older.*

"All right then," said Miss Mickle. "Think of algebra as a game full of puzzles, which are interesting to figure out. I promise we'll have fun together. Now, when you are finished signing your books, you can go on to your next class."

Latin was taught by Mr. Roscoe, an elderly white-haired man with a very red face and a slow manner of talking that Ida found irritating. He gave out a textbook called *Elementary Latin*, by Ullman and Henry.

Ida read the first paragraph and discovered that Latin was not a place, but the language the ancient Romans spoke.

There, I've already learned something.

Next came study hall, which turned out to be in the same room. The teacher left, as did some students. Other students came in.

A woman entered and went to the front desk. "In this period," she said, "you're free to study or do homework. Not today, of course, though you might look at your new textbooks. In a short while, you'll go on to your next class." She gestured toward a clock on the wall. "Don't lose track of time."

Ida turned to Dot. "Where did you go to school before? I went to a one-room school up in Elk Valley."

"I had regular school in Oak Creek."

"No high school there?" Ida asked.

Ida saw a flash of unease on Dot's face. "I . . . I wanted to come here." She added quickly, "I read a lot."

Accepting the change of subject, Ida asked, "What do you read?"

"Whatever I can. It lets me be alone," Dot said.

"Back home we don't have many books," Ida confessed. "I like to read, so I want to do better."

"I read every book in my old school," said Dot. "But Oak Creek doesn't have a library. Then I heard that Steamboat does. One day the train stopped near where I was standing. I called up to the engineer—it just popped into my head— if he—his name is Mr. Whitcombe—could take me to the Steamboat library. He laughed and said, 'Why not? Climb aboard.' That's when I started to use the train."

Ida only said, "I've never been on one."

"Never?"

Ida shook her head.

Dot said, "I think of the locomotive as a fire-breathing dragon. I love fairy tales." She glanced at the clock. "Next class," she announced.

Miss Castle taught the English class. She was a small, stout woman, wearing a long skirt. Her gray hair, parted in the middle, was tied up in a bun. Her deep eyes, thought Ida, were pretty.

"Good morning," she said in a surprisingly sweet voice. "My name is Miss Castle. This is English One. I've been teaching for fifteen years.

The best way to tell you what this class is about is to read you a poem." Holding the book open before her with two hands, like it was a hymnal, she read:

> *"He ate and drank the precious words,*
> *His spirit grew robust;*
> *He knew no more that he was poor,*
> *Nor that his frame was dust.*
> *He danced along the dingy days,*
> *And this bequest of wings*
> *Was but a book. What liberty*
> *A loosened spirit brings!*

"That was written by Miss Emily Dickinson," Miss Castle continued. "Our best American poet. I so admire that poem. If I can bring you to a deep fondness for literature, and thereby bring you loosened spirits, we shall have done well."

Ida was sure she was going to like Miss Castle and English.

The teacher handed out the textbook, *Studies in English-World Literature*, by Ottis Bedney Sperlin. Then the class was over.

Ida said to Dot, "With all your reading, you're going to love this class."

"I did like that poem," said Dot, checking the schedule. "Oh, good. Lunchtime. I'm starved. Do you want to eat together?"

Ida's heart sank. She had brought no lunch. *I'm doing everything wrong*, she thought. *No certificate, nothing to write with, and I didn't even think about lunch! Maybe I don't belong in high school.*

"Did you forget lunch?" said Dot, reacting to the look on Ida's face. "You can share mine. First days are hard! I'm sure you'll remember your lunch tomorrow."

"Thank you," said Ida, deciding she liked Dot.

They asked an older-looking student where they were supposed to eat and learned they could go outside.

When they went out of the building, a number of students were already sitting on the grass.

Dot found an open spot and plopped down cross-legged. She opened her cloth bag and pulled out a sandwich wrapped in newspaper.

"Hope you like cheese," she said, handing half to Ida, whose stomach suddenly reminded her she had skipped breakfast. Dot also shared her apple. Finally, she brought up a bottle of Nehi peach soda pop. "We can split it," she said, twisting off the cap.

"What is it?"

"Soda. Haven't you ever had it? Go on, taste it."

Ida took a sip. It made her mouth sweet and tingly. "Nice," she said. Between the food and Dot's kindness, Ida's mood was settling, and her enthusiasm was returning.

"Hey, babes!"

Ida looked up. It was that girl again, Lulu.

"Can I join you Janes?"

"Sure," said Ida, glad to see Lulu. With a gesture toward Dot, she said, "This is Dorothy Kovács. Lulu Gallagher. We're all new here."

"Ducky to meet you," said Lulu as she dropped down. "Are you feeling better since this morning?" she asked Ida.

"Much, thanks."

Dot said, "Is your name really Lulu?"

"Actually, it's Louise, but everyone calls me Lulu. I love it because do you know what else it means?"

Both Ida and Dot shook their heads.

"A gangster's sweetheart."

"I never heard that," said Ida, smiling at the absurdity. "How do you find new words?"

Dot said, "Reading books, I'd guess."

"Not me," said Lulu. "Hate reading books.

Prune pits. Love magazines. You know, *True Con-fessions*. And *Flapper*. Only twenty cents. *Flapper* lists all the new words. Know what it says on its cover? 'Not for Old Fogies.' I love that mag."

Ida turned to Dot. "Lulu likes parties, too."

"They're the bee's knees," agreed Lulu.

Ida gave her a questioning look.

"Means something good."

Dot said, "My favorite new phrase is 'heebie-jeebies.'"

"What's that?" asked Ida.

"The jitters," said Lulu.

"When I was coming this morning," said Dot, "thinking about starting high school, I was full of the heebie-jeebies."

For the first time that morning, Ida laughed. "So was I!" She was relieved to know she wasn't the only one who had been nervous. "'Heebie-jeebies' describes the feeling perfectly. I like it!"

Lulu jumped up. "I haven't forgotten about making a club, but I need to find someone who is having a party. Copacetic. I love cutting a rug."

"What's cutting a rug?" called Ida.

"Dancing," said Lulu as she rushed off.

Ida, smiling, turned to Dot. "Even though I

don't understand her most of the time, I love the way she talks. She's fun. What's . . . 'copacetic'?"

"Means good. Did you like our teachers?" asked Dot.

"Miss Castle. And especially that Miss Mickle. In my old school, we had only one teacher. Here, I'll get to know a bunch."

"It's all so new," agreed Dot. After a moment, she asked, "Have you ever done anything unusual?"

"Back home, I drove our car to get to school."

"By yourself?"

"With my brother. He did the brakes."

"Wow! How old are you?"

"Fourteen."

"Same. We don't have a car. Too expensive. My brother told me a new Ford costs two hundred and sixty dollars."

When classes resumed, there was science, taught by a Mr. Hanson. He was a tall, broad-shouldered man who seemed to be bursting out of his suit. He spoke so fast that for the most part Ida didn't know what he was talking about. *There's so much to get used to.*

The final class of the day was music, with

Miss Mickle again. This time she offered no text-book. But on her desk was something Ida had never seen before: it was a box, like a small suitcase, with a crank sticking out the front side.

After introducing herself, Miss Mickle said, "To begin, I'd like you to listen to this Silvertone phonograph. It plays music." She unlatched the top of the wooden box and flipped up a lid. "I'm sure you've seen others like it."

Ida had heard phonographic music played when she and Ma had visited the Steamboat Mercantile general store. And Tom had talked about the machines. Eager to listen, she leaned forward in anticipation.

Miss Mickle turned the crank on the box, then flicked a switch. A disc on top began to spin. As Ida watched, the teacher lifted a metal arm that was attached to the box and set it down on the spinning disc.

"Let's first listen to Ludwig van Beethoven, a German composer who lived a hundred years ago. Here is the way his Fifth Symphony begins."

As the music thundered, a startled Ida felt the sound flow over her like a wave of deep emotion. It thrilled her.

After a few minutes, Miss Mickle lifted the

needle, took the record off, and replaced it with another.

"Now here," she announced, "is Mr. Eddie Cantor singing a brand-new recording."

A raucous, metallic voice blared forth; the song was bouncy, rhythmical, exciting.

> *"If you knew Susie, like I know Susie*
> *Oh! Oh! Oh! What a girl*
> *There's none so classy*
> *As this fair lassie*
> *Oh! Oh! Holy Moses, what a chassis!"*

The song went on for another three minutes while Miss Mickle smiled and clicked her fingers loudly to the rhythm.

The whole classroom was full of laughing, grinning students. Ida, used to hymns and folk music, had never heard anything like it, and she grinned too. So did Dot.

When the song was over, the class applauded wildly.

"The first selection was what we call classical music. The second, popular music," said Miss Mickle. "We'll listen to all kinds of music. From trendy to classical. Now I'm going to play, and get you to sing along with, Mr. R. Gunnar, as he does 'Ain't We Got Fun?'"

"Ain't we got fun?
Not much money, oh, but honey
Ain't we got fun?
The rent's unpaid, dear
We haven't a car
But in any way, dear
We'll stay as we are
Even if we owe the grocer
Don't we have fun?
Tax collector's getting closer
Still, we have fun!
There's nothing surer
The rich get rich, and the poor get poorer
In the meantime, in between time
Ain't we got fun?"

"I urge you to memorize that," said Miss Mickle with her bright smile. "It'll help soothe all your worries. And do learn to snap your fingers. Snaps will keep you on rhythm no matter what kind of music we hear."

The class applauded again. There were even a few clicking fingers.

At twelve thirty, school was dismissed. "I love that Miss Mickle," exclaimed Ida. "She's so full of . . ."

"Zoom," suggested Dot.

Ida laughed. "That sounds right. When I get to be a teacher, I want to be like her. Which means I have to learn that song. And that machine—I heard a phonograph before, but nothing like that."

"Sorry," said Dot. "I have to catch the one thirty. Don't want to miss it. Ida, I'm so glad we met. Gosh, it's the cat's pajamas to have met you on my first day. Can I be your friend?"

"Copacetic," said Ida with a grin.

"See you tomorrow!" cried Dot as she hurried away.

Ida walked down the main hallway, enjoying being among so many students. She saw the man who had been greeting the entering kids that morning. As she passed him, he called out, "Miss Bidson!"

Taken by surprise, Ida stopped and looked at him.

"I'm Mr. Langly. The school principal here. I believe you are boarding with Miss Sedgewick. She's told me all about you. Described you very well."

75

"Yes, sir."

"I gather she met you at that tiny one-room school up in Elk Valley. Miss Bidson, I'm sure she told you we keep extremely high academic standards. Considering your background, you may find things a bit difficult here. Perfectly understandable. Don't take it too hard if you do. Many of our more rural students find high school isn't right for them. We understand." He offered a thin smile.

Taken aback, Ida looked up at him and thought, *Why did he say that?* In the face of his blandness, she felt obliged to say "Thank you," then she stepped out of the school.

Ida blinked in the sunlight as she emerged from the building. She remembered the doubts she'd felt earlier, and how they'd given way as the day had progressed. She had made a friend and was already learning new things—that last class with Miss Mickle had even been fun! *Never mind what the principal thinks*, she told herself. He didn't know her, and she would show him that she *did* belong here. Putting Mr. Langly's words out of mind, she said, "I did it! My first day."

Arms wrapped around her textbooks, she

made her way back to Trudy's house, relieved she didn't get lost. She was so glad she hadn't left school over the certificate mix-up. She had saved herself—she was sure—from spending a life milking Bluebell.

She couldn't wait for tomorrow.

In her room, Ida spread out her textbooks on the bed. The one she found most interesting was the Latin book, with its many illustrations, some in color. The way people looked and dressed told her how different the ancient world was.

Back home I was in another world, too. Home feels not twenty miles away, but thousands. It's all so new here. It's the modern world, she told herself, and tried—and failed—some finger clicks.

She turned to her algebra book and randomly opened it to page five:

The figure at the right is a rectangular parallelopiped. You know that its volume equals its length multiplied by its width, multiplied by its height. If the length, width, and height are represented by l, w, and h, respectively, and the volume by V, then write the formula for the volume.

"Ugh," said Ida, and snapped the book shut. She picked up her English textbook and opened it by chance to a poem.

Sea-Fever
John Masefield

I must go down to the seas again, to the lonely
  sea and the sky,
And all I ask is a tall ship and a star to steer
  her by;
And the wheel's kick and the wind's song and
  the white sail's shaking,
And a grey mist on the sea's face, and a grey
  dawn breaking.

With a shiver of delight, Ida sighed, closed her eyes, and tried to imagine the sea. "Someday I'll go there, too," she whispered to herself.

SEVEN

Not wanting to make Trudy feel bad, Ida didn't mention anything about the registration mix-up. She was happy to throw it—along with her other first-day heebie-jeebies—away as a bad memory. In any case, with classes running smoothly all week, Ida enjoyed getting used to the rhythm of the days. Most of all she was loving school.

Algebra seemed to consist of—as Miss Mickle had promised—puzzles, and although Ida found them perplexing, she thought them interesting, a kind of mystery language. Besides, the always cheerful Miss Mickle was full of good humor and explained things so well they seemed entertaining.

Latin, with the very formal Mr. Roscoe, was strange with its list of words she needed to learn. *Fortuna, via, magna, nova.* Ida struggled to understand what the nominative case—the subject of a verb—was. Fortunately, she remembered that a verb was a word that showed an action or a feeling. But Latin seemed to mostly consist of memorizing, and Ida was good at that.

In English, Miss Castle set the students to learn a poem written by someone named Austin Dobson, who, the teacher informed them, "ranks high as a writer of graceful society verse." She read one of Mr. Dobson's poems from their textbook:

> *"In a work-a-day world—for its needs and*
> *woes,*
> *There is place and enough for the pains of*
> *prose;*
> *But whenever the May-bells clash and chime,*
> *Then hey! For the ripple of laughing rhyme!"*

Ida thought the poem simple but liked how it sounded sort of bouncy. She thought more of it when Miss Castle explained that the word "prose" meant nothing less than the way people spoke normally. Ida enjoyed the idea that she spoke *prose* but had never known it before.

"We'll do a good deal of memorizing in this class," Miss Castle explained. "I hope it will help with your writing. And speaking of hope, please memorize this:

"Hope is the thing with feathers—
That perches in the soul—
And sings the tune without the words—
And never stops—at all.

"That's also by my favorite, Miss Dickinson."

That notion of hope pleased Ida so much that she wrote out the poem's words.

As for science, it was a struggle to understand, but Ida worked hard, dumbfounded to learn all kinds of things about her insides, such as that her heart had four chambers.

Maybe, Ida mused, *high school is learning things about yourself that you never knew before.*

What don't I know about myself? she wondered.

A lot, came the answer.

Since she and Dot shared the same schedule, they remained together, and never lost their way, and always took desks next to one another, usually at the back of the room. Whenever they could—and sometimes when they weren't supposed to—they chattered. Ida was delighted by how many things there were to talk about: Her family, Ma, Pa, Felix, even the baby. The ranch. Her cow. How she drove to school. Trudy's house. She told Dot about her old school and how she had secretly been the teacher there for six weeks.

"You've done so many daring things," said Dot, which pleased Ida, though she tried not to show it.

"Sounds like your home is happy," Dot said.

"Very," answered Ida.

Dot talked nothing about her family and mostly about what she had read, including her two favorite books, *The Wizard of Oz* and *Little Women*. "*Little Women* is about these sisters and their wonderful family. I wish I could live like that. *The Wizard of Oz* has a girl named Dorothy going to a magical place where Glinda the Good Witch lives. Did you know there can be good witches? Maybe I'll become one."

"When I'm done with high school," Ida said, "I'm going to a faraway college so I can be a real teacher. What do you want to do?"

"Don't really know," Dot confessed.

"Be a teacher, like me."

"I don't like people enough."

Ida, remembering that poem about hope, asked, "What would be your best hope?"

Dot grew thoughtful. "I guess I'd like to travel."

"Where?"

"Someplace where no one could find me."

"Why?"

"Just would."

When Ida thought about what Dot said, she was sure there was something wrong in her new friend's life, but she didn't want to ask.

The fact was, everything was going swell for Ida, and she wanted to keep it that way.

EIGHT

ⵠ

ON FRIDAY AFTERNOON, Ida stepped into a
deserted house. With Trudy not there, the rooms
seemed bigger, quieter, and neater. Unlike when
Ida returned to her log cabin home from her
one-room school, there was no one with whom
to talk. No Ma, no Pa, no Felix or Shelby. No
Teddy. No Bluebell. Not even chickens. But after
a crowded week at school, Ida found herself lik-
ing the private quiet. It was good to be just by
herself. She did feel a pang of guilt that she had
no chores to do. Then she reminded herself she
did have a chore: studying.

That night for dinner, Trudy served a dish that

was rice mixed with green peppers and onions, along with grated cheese.

"As you can see," she said, "it's topped with canned tomato sauce, baked, and then slices of a hard-cooked egg are added. It's called 'à la Milanese.'"

"What does 'à la' mean?"

"Means made in the style of a person or place—*à la* Trudy. Or *à la* Milan—a place in Italy."

Remembering the atlas, Ida had a vague conception that Italy was a country in Europe but didn't want to show her ignorance by asking.

"The recipe is from my Boston cookbook. Do you like it?"

"Oh yes," said Ida, wishing to be polite as she reminded herself that Boston was where the American Revolution began.

Trudy said, "Well, your first week is behind you. Tell me what you think of it all."

Ida described her classes. "Latin is a language, not a place. And of all my teachers, I like that Miss Mickle the best."

"She's new," said Trudy. "I'm afraid I haven't spent time with her yet. It can take a while for new teachers to settle in."

"Settle in?"

"Learn how we do things here."

"How come all the lady teachers are 'miss'?"

"Mr. Langly—the principal—thinks married women don't make good teachers."

"Why?" cried Ida.

"I'm afraid he's not fond of modern women," said Trudy.

"But . . . that doesn't seem right," said Ida.

"Well, it's pretty much the way schools are run," said Trudy. Clearly wanting to change the subject, she asked, "Have you made any friends?"

"The best is Dorothy. Dot. She's from a place called Oak Creek."

"Oh dear," said Trudy with a frown. "A lot of coal miners live there. What's her last name?"

"Kovács."

"Hmm. Many of those miners are immigrants. Though there's all kinds of prejudice against them, the mines bring them in. Why does she come to Steamboat for school?"

"Don't know. We've become good friends. She gets to school by train."

"Does she! How unusual."

"And then there's Lulu."

"Is she that fast-talking rude girl? Ida, I do hope she hasn't become a friend."

Unsettled, Ida said, "I . . . I sort of like her."

"Ida, having suitable friends helps."

"Helps with what?"

"The way people think about you."

"I think most people like me. And I haven't met any bad kids."

"Well . . ." Trudy began, only to pause. "The important thing—when you choose friends—is that your friends will be liked too."

"What do you mean?"

"I hate to say it, but, as I am acting as your guardian, the way people judge you and your friends reflects on me, too."

"I don't understand."

"Ida, I'm your guardian. I have to think of my own reputation. And protect myself. No one else will."

Ida was taken aback. It was not something she had ever thought about. "Have . . . have I done something wrong?"

"Not yet," said Trudy with a laugh, seemingly trying to make light of it.

Ida didn't know how to respond. A moment

went by, then she decided to try changing the subject, as Trudy had done earlier. "Do you have some needle and thread?"

"Did something tear?" Trudy sounded relieved to move to a new topic.

"I want to make my dresses a little . . . shorter."

Worry lines appeared on Trudy's face. "How short?"

Ida spoke cautiously. "Just a little."

"As long as they're not too short, I can help."

"Four inches," Ida suggested.

"Let's do two," said Trudy with a forced smile.

After dinner, Ida stood in the middle of the living room while Trudy pinned her dress hems higher all around.

"Are you finding classes difficult?" Trudy asked.

"Not really."

"They are a long way off," said Trudy as she continued pinning Ida's dress, "but I suppose I should remind you about your November grades. Those midterm results are important. A fair number of students from one-room schools around the county don't do well. They're not encouraged to come back after the midterm holiday."

Ida remembered what the principal had said

to her. *She's telling me she's worried I won't do well and won't stay in school.* "Do you know what my pa likes to say?" Ida said. "'Work, not wishes, whips the job.'"

"I like that," said Trudy.

Back in her room, Ida stitched her dresses—three inches shorter—beneath the light of the electric bulb. As she did, she thought about all that had happened that week. The school. The different teachers. Yes, if she could be a teacher, she *would* be like Miss Mickle. But did all women teachers have to stay unmarried? She tried to think of herself as married. She couldn't. Instead, she thought about Dot, her new friend, and Lulu.

I don't care what Trudy says: Lulu is fun. I'm not going to let Trudy pick my friends.

And—"copacetic," "heebie-jeebies"—new words and phrases. New ideas. She liked them a lot. She recalled that poem about poetry and "Sea-Fever."

Her mind went back to something Trudy had said: "It's always best to be content with what you have." *Trudy seems almost timid. I don't think I want to be like her. And my parents tell me what's right,* she thought, *not Miss Sedgewick.*

Suddenly yawning, Ida got into her night-gown, turned off the light, and climbed into bed.

I didn't study, she berated herself. *But so much has happened this week.* She tried—and failed—a few finger snaps.

Tomorrow I'll have all day to study.

She pulled the quilt up to her chin and snuggled down, only to have another new thought: *I'm going to change. Become different.*

As Ida drifted off to sleep, a notion came into her head: *How strange to think I'm going to be different. And I don't even know how.*

I can't wait! she told herself.

NINE

At Monday morning homeroom, Ida greeted Dot like an old friend and was met with the same enthusiasm. It made Ida feel a part of the school. As they had come to do for all their classes, they sat next to each other.

Miss Blake called the students to order and began taking attendance. The next moment, the classroom door opened and in walked Mr. Langly.

Miss Blake immediately stopped what she was doing and stood up.

"Mr. Langly," she said, by way of greeting. "Welcome. Students, for those of you who haven't met him, this is Mr. Langly, our principal."

Mr. Langly did no more than nod at the teacher, then stood before her desk. To Ida's eyes, he looked stern.

"Greetings," said the principal. "I wanted to take a moment to welcome all newcomers to Steamboat Springs High School. Since we are Routt County's best high school, we expect each and every one of you to live up to our high standards and do the town proud. As you should know, Routt County was named after Edward Routt, the first governor of our state, a man who believed in hard work, fairness, and superior morals. I expect no less from each of you. What is more—"

Ida had raised her hand.

Mr. Langly, seeming surprised, looked at her severely. "Yes, Miss Bidson, is something the matter?"

Ida, encouraged that he remembered her, stood up. "Please, sir, I think that governor's name was *John Long* Routt."

Mr. Langly's pale cheeks grew pink. In the room, there was absolute silence.

"Miss Bidson, I believe I'm in a better position

to know the facts. May I suggest you are *not* in Steamboat High to correct your betters, but to learn. Please be seated."

Ida, stung by the principal's sharpness, dropped down into her seat.

Mr. Langly stood still for a moment. Then he turned to the teacher. "Thank you, Miss Blake. That will be all."

With that, he marched out of the room and shut the door loudly behind him.

The silence in the classroom was intense. A few students glanced at Ida. It was Miss Blake who finally spoke. "Miss Bidson, that was very rude—"

"I just—"

"May I give you some advice, Miss Bidson: do *not* make yourself an adversary of our principal."

"But—"

"No more, Miss Bidson. Class dismissed."

Ida and Dot went out of the room, Ida thinking, *That Mr. Langly was wrong. Pa always likes hearing new facts from me. But I suppose I shouldn't have said that. Maybe it's not*—she recalled Trudy's word—*proper here.*

"What's 'adversary' mean?" she asked Dot.

"An enemy."

"Do you think," said Ida, "I'll get in trouble with Mr. Langly for saying what I did?"

"That'd be awful" was all Dot would say.

Ida resolved to steer clear of the principal from then on.

TEN

THE TUESDAY LUNCH PERIOD was almost over when Lulu rushed up to Ida and Dot.

"I found someone who is having a party!"

"Who?"

"Some boy. A senior. I don't really know him. But I'm going. Saturday night. Don't care what my old man says. And I have a great buzz for that club I'm going to make."

"What's a buzz?" asked Ida.

"An idea," explained Dot.

"Can you tell us what it is?"

"Need to get everything set. And I want to get more people for it. Spill you later."

"Can't wait," said Ida.

"Ducky," said Lulu. "Meet today after school. Room 218. You have to come. Will you?"

"I want to," said Ida, laughing. As Lulu ran off, Ida turned to Dot. "Lulu's idea is bound to be unusual. It'll be fun to do something a little daring."

Their last class was music, during which Miss Mickle explained the basic notes of the C scale and used a xylophone to sound it out.

When class was over, Ida and Dot stood in the rapidly emptying hallway. Ida said, "Let's go to Lulu's meeting. See what kind of club she's inventing."

They made their way to room 218. It was a regular classroom, but no one was there.

"Wonder if anyone will come," said Dot.

Even as she spoke, a girl walked in. "Is this Lulu's club?"

"That's why we're here," said Ida. "I'm Ida. This is Dot."

"I'm Becky," said the girl.

Ida remembered Becky had stood behind her in the registration line.

Another girl poked her head into the room. "Is this where that Lulu said to meet?" she asked.

"Yes," said Becky.

"I'm Helene."

Ida thought Helene was pretty but dressed in a disorderly fashion, with the hem of her skirt lopsided, a button undone, and a smudge on her white collar. Even her hair was mussed. It was as if she and her clothing were going in different directions.

"What are your names?" Helene asked, her voice small.

"Ida."

"Dot."

"Becky."

"First year?" asked Helene of all.

They nodded.

"Oh, good," said Becky. "I'm tired of being the only one not knowing things."

"Now we can not know together," said Ida.

They all laughed.

"I get so mixed up about where to go," said Helene. "You know, jingle-brained."

"Jingle-brained," cried Becky. "Perfect description."

As Becky spoke, Lulu burst in. "Sorry I'm late. I was trying to get some more people for the club, but I couldn't get anyone else. I told some boy we were going to have a club, and he said it was a dumb idea. Thick, right? So, I told him that boys who think clubs are dumb are dodos."

"What are dodos?" asked Ida.

"Dead birds. Or people who hate swell things. So, this is just going to be a girls' club."

"To do what?" said Helene.

"Here's my idea," said Lulu. "We're all girls. All first year, right? So, that's the club. A first-year-girls' club."

"But what are we going to *do*?" asked Becky.

"Newcomers have to stick together," said Lulu. "My father is in the Rotary Club with Mr. Langly, our principal. It was Langly who got my old man to move his business to Steamboat. That's the way clubs work. Members help each other. So, first, we'll be best friends and have fun. Okay, here's my swanky idea. Every week a new girl gets to be president, and that girl gets to pick what we do. Then, no matter what, we have to do it."

No one objected.

"Does our club have a name?" asked Helene. "Like Rotary?"

"Do we need one?" Becky asked.

"Ab-so-lute-ly," said Lulu. "Clubs must have

names. Rotary. Moose. Odd Fellows. We have to have one."

Helene said, "Okay, then, what about Odd Girls?"

"I don't want to be odd," said Dot.

"In Steamboat," said Becky, "all the sports teams are called 'sailors.' But I don't think there are any lady sailors."

There was more silence while they all thought about it.

Helene said, "What about Steamboat Sister Sailors?"

Lulu objected: "She just said there are no girl sailors."

"Maybe there are some secret ones," suggested Dot.

There was silence until Ida said, "I know. How about Secret Sisters?"

"Snuggle pup's bow-how!" cried Lulu. "That's the best berries. I love secrets. We'll be the Secret Sisters."

Everyone laughed and clapped their hands.

"Now what?" asked Helene.

Lulu pointed to Ida. "Since you thought up our name, you be the first president. We'll have a start-off meeting this coming Thursday afternoon." To Ida, she added, "So, you need to bring an idea for what we're going to do."

At dinner that night, Ida told Trudy about the meeting.

"What kind of club is it?"

"Each week a new girl is president, and she chooses something different to do," said Ida, not altogether sure she understood what it all meant. "I'm the first president."

"What do you call yourselves?"

"The Secret Sisters."

"Secret? Oh dear. That sounds as if you are hiding something."

"It's because we're not really sisters."

"Is that Lulu in it?"

Ida nodded.

"Was that name Lulu's idea?" asked Trudy.

"It was mine."

"Well, I must say, I just hope you keep things respectable."

She's always worried something bad will happen, thought Ida, but she didn't say it aloud.

After a pause, Trudy said, "Ida, dear, speaking of being respectable, at school today I heard that—yesterday—you got into a bit of a dust-up with Mr. Langly."

"What's a . . . dust-up?"

"An argument."

"I didn't!" cried Ida, instantly remembering. "He . . . he came to class and said something . . . that was wrong."

"Wrong?"

"Not right."

"What did you do?"

"I told him . . . what was right."

"Goodness. You *are* bold. Did he ask you to?"

"No."

Trudy became silent and then said, "Ida, Mr. Langly is the head of the school. He runs it quite well. But . . . but you need to know that he doesn't like to be . . . corrected."

"I only—"

"Ida, I need to give you some friendly advice. Do *not* cross Mr. Langly."

"He told me he doesn't think that I'm smart enough to be at the high school."

"He did? When was that?"

Ida recounted her hallway meeting with the principal. "He said I might find things difficult here."

"Oh dear. He's so protective of the school's reputation. Wants it to be a top school. Maybe he was just trying to give you a word of warning. To get you to work hard. But I admit, what he said wasn't nice."

"Did you tell him I was a teacher—for a while?"

Trudy shook her head. "I'm afraid he wouldn't have approved, so I never told him. In fact, now that you mention it, you mustn't tell anyone about that. I . . . I was taking a chance."

"On what?"

"You."

"Oh."

Fidgeting with her fork, Trudy was silent for a few moments. Ida, sure Trudy was going to say more, waited. "It's just that," Trudy began, "Mr. Langly, while he believes strongly in education, doesn't care for what people call 'modern.' Seems to be offended by it. If he disapproves of a student's performance or behavior, as principal, he may tell them to leave and never come back. It doesn't happen too often, but please do be careful."

"I'll try," said Ida uneasily.

Trudy smiled and changed the subject, which Ida had learned she did when she felt uncomfortable. "Well, I must say, I don't think you have any idea how much pleasure I get from sharing dinner with you every night. And . . . chatting. Living alone can be . . ." She did not finish her thought.

But Ida did: *Lonely.*

That night, after washing the dinner dishes, Ida worked through the homework she had been assigned, reading a chapter on poetry in her English book and deciding she liked poetry. She also read a chapter in Latin. But as she got ready for bed, she was thinking about the Secret Sisters club. The more she considered it, the more she liked it. *I've never done anything like this in my whole life. "Snuggle pup's bow-how." What did that mean? I'll have to ask Dot. It's so good to have smart friends. As for Trudy's objection to the club—it seems silly. But that warning about Mr. Langly. That's the second time I've been told to be careful of him. Could he really make me leave school just because I know the name of the first governor of Colorado? That's silly too.*

Ida tried to recall that song Miss Mickle played:

Ain't we got fun?
Not much money, oh, but honey
Ain't we got fun?

Before getting into bed, Ida stood in front of the mirror and brushed out her hair. She missed the pull of Ma's fingers twisting it into braids. *I'm the only one of the Sisters with pigtails. All the others have bobbed hair. The modern way.*

That gave her an idea of what to do with the Secret Sisters. *I wonder what Trudy will say.*

Then, as she dropped off to sleep, she again remembered Trudy's warning about Mr. Langly. And about Lulu. Because that was what they were, warnings.

I need to continue to keep away from Mr. Langly, she told herself. *That shouldn't be hard. Lulu said he's her father's friend, but I don't care. I like Lulu. She's fun. And modern. As for Trudy . . . I mustn't get her in trouble. Pa's right: I'm only here because Trudy is letting me stay with her. I must be careful.*

The next day, when walking to class with Dot, Ida saw Mr. Langly at the end of the hall.

"Let's go down here," she said, pulling Dot along with her.

"Why?" asked Dot.

"The principal. Remember, I corrected him? Miss Sedgewick said I need to be careful of him, so I'm staying out of his way."

"What might he do?" asked Dot, looking back at Mr. Langly.

Make me leave school, Ida thought. But all she said was "I don't want to find out. Come on."

ELEVEN

～

Dear Ma and Pa and Felix and Shelby and
Snooker and Bluebell and Teddy, and the sheep,
and all the chickens,

Salvo (that's "hello" in Latin).

I miss you!!!

Life in Steamboat is _so_ different. I love it. Miss
Sedgewick—Trudy—tries to be helpful. She gave
me the two-cent stamp and envelope for this letter
and will show me where to find the post office.

I have five classes. I like music and English
the best. Science the least. The teacher talks too
fast. Mathematics is fun, but hard. I understand
why I study Latin. Mr. Roscoe said it will help

with my writing. But guess what? There is no such place as Latin. It's just an old language. But guess what again? Lots of English words are Latin words! Like "agenda" and "naïve." I didn't even know them in English before. But they're from Latin!

I have new friends. Dot—Dorothy—is my best friend. She is the cat's pajamas. Girls talk that way here. It means she's great! Dot lives in Oak Creek and comes to school every day on a <u>train</u>! In the engineer's cab!!! She said that someday she will invite me for an overnight visit, so I will ride the train!

That will be so tasty.

That's something else people say.

Lulu, another new friend, is what people call a live wire. She talks flapper. It's like a new language. So, I'm learning different ways of talking, old and new. It's saggio ("wise" in Latin), even though sometimes I'm naïve.

Guess what else? I am in a club. A club is a group of friends who get together to do something and help each other, except we don't know what we'll do yet. Our club's name is the Secret Sisters. It's Lulu's club, but I thought up the name. There are five girls in our club. Each week we have a new president. Guess what again? I'm president number one!

(Did you know that the president of the United States, Calvin Coolidge, is number 30?)

Tomorrow—our first meeting—I have to think of what we will do. I have an idea that I think will surprise everyone.

Even you.

I like having friends. Can I be my own friend? Is that silly? I am not very tall, but I am curious about things. I am always asking why.

<u>Why</u> do I do that? Ha ha!

(That was an iocus! "Joke" in Latin.)

Guess what? I am writing this in prose.

And I like poetry more than ever. It's . . . like drinking cool water on a muggy day.

That is my news.

Love you and miss you all.

Thank you for letting me go to high school!! I will always, always, always do my best.

Vale (that's "goodbye" in Latin),
Ida Bidson
Your filia and soro ("daughter" and "sister" in Latin), aeternum ("forever").

TWELVE

THE SECRET SISTERS had gathered at the back of an empty second-floor classroom for lunch. It was Lulu who said, "Okay, Ida, you're the first president."

Everyone applauded.

"What are we going to do?"

"I've been thinking," Ida began.

Everyone applauded again. "Go on," said Lulu.

Now that it was time to share her idea, Ida was surprised to find herself a bit reluctant to say it aloud. "What I thought," she said slowly, "was that all of you have bobbed hair, except me. Just braids."

"Right," said Helene. "Absolutely prune pit."

"Wurp style," added Lulu.

"Sinker," added Becky.

"Do you think so?" asked Ida. She had not expected such a strong response.

"You're the only one of us who looks different," said Lulu.

"My idea," said Ida, feeling increasing unease but forcing herself to barrel ahead, "is to cut my hair."

Applause.

Becky said, "Hank's Hair is next to Light's Clothing on Lincoln. He does ladies' hair."

"We'll go with you," said Lulu. "Today. Right after school. We'll have a hair party."

"Hair today, gone tomorrow," cried Helene.

Everyone laughed except Ida, who fingered her braids and thought that maybe her great idea wasn't so great. She hadn't expected things to move so fast.

She looked to Dot, who had remained silent.

"Be ritzy," exclaimed Lulu, trying to get Ida to share their enthusiasm. "Pigtails. You don't want to have hair like a pig, do you?"

"Right," pressed Becky. "You have to do it!"

"How much does it cost?" asked Ida, now

trying to think of a way out.

"Can't be more than a dollar."

"I don't have that," said Ida, knowing it wasn't exactly true.

"We'll all chip in," said Becky. "Right?"

"No," said Helene. "We'll all *clip* in."

Laughter.

"Actually, I'm not sure what my mother would say," Ida tried.

"She lives up in North Routt, right?" Becky said. "That's twenty miles away."

"The woman you board with, Miss Sedgewick," said Lulu. "I've seen her. She has bobbed hair."

"Anyway," said Becky, "we all agreed to do whatever the weekly president suggested. And you suggested it."

"Won't take even an hour. That Hank Penderby works fast," said Helene.

As Ida sat there silently—everyone looking at her—she glanced at Dot. Dot seemed worried and still hadn't said anything.

"Today?" Ida said to the group, in a weak voice. The idea had seemed exciting the other night, but now that it was happening, she was sorry she had suggested it.

"Right after school," said Lulu. "Whoopee time."

"Anyway," said Becky, "your head will be lighter."

"A bubblehead," cried Helene.

Ida looked down at her hands. It was clear that everyone—except perhaps Dot—wanted her to do it. Maybe it would be a good thing to look like everyone else. To be in fashion. To be modern. "All right," she said, not with a lot of certainty.

Everyone—again except for Dot—clapped their hands.

"You really want to do this?" Dot asked Ida as they went back to class. "I like your braids."

"I . . . I guess so," Ida heard herself say.

"You don't have to," Dot said.

"I said I would," returned Ida.

In music class, Miss Mickle held up pictures of various instruments. A violin. A cornet. And more. For each one, she played a bit of recorded music on her phonograph machine so the class might learn what kind of sound the instrument made.

Ida was not listening or paying much attention to what the teacher was saying. Or playing. Fingering one of her braids, she kept thinking about the haircut. She was also studying Miss Mickle's bobbed hair. The teacher was pretty, and she was Ida's favorite. Ida wished she could look like her. *Then I'll do it*, she told herself, and flicked her braids behind her neck as if to get rid of them.

After school, the Sisters walked down Pine Street. Ida was in the middle, surrounded, almost as if to make sure she would not run away. It made her feel like she was a prisoner.

Nervous, she kept wondering what her mother—and Trudy—would say. Then she told herself she was grown-up enough to make her own decisions about such important matters. But she would save the ribbons her mother used. Her hair could always grow back.

With Lulu leading the way, they soon reached Lincoln Avenue and turned right. Hank's Hair was a narrow little shop next to Light's clothing store. On the sidewalk by the door, a thick pole on a pedestal was painted red, white, and blue. The words "Hank's Hair," in old-fashioned letters, were on the door's window.

"*Hair* we are," said Helene.

The Secret Sisters walked in.

The barbershop was a small room dominated by a large chair with a footrest, headrest, and leather cushions. The chair was on a stand that could rotate. Large mirrors hung on either side of the room. Behind the chair was a table upon which sat all kinds of colored bottles.

Seated in the chair, legs crossed, was Mr. Hank Penderby, the barber. He was a mostly bald man with a great droopy mustache. He was reading a magazine.

As the Sisters entered, he sat up. "Yes, girls, what can I do for you?"

Helene took Ida by the arm and eased her forward. "She wants her hair cut. Bobbed."

"Does she?" the barber asked, a bemused look on his face.

Ida stood there, not knowing what to say.

"Ab-so-lute-ly," Lulu called out.

"Now, I just want to make sure I have this right." Mr. Penderby was looking at Ida. "We're cutting off *your* pretty braids?"

"Yes, sir."

The girls applauded.

"And your mother?" asked the barber. "What does she say?"

"She's up in North Routt," Ida whispered.

"Are you boarding?"

"With Miss Gertrude Sedgewick."

"Well, all right then," said Mr. Penderby. "I

do her hair." He climbed out of the chair and patted the seat. "You can sit right up here, young lady."

Ida went forward, stepped on the footrest, and, with a helping hand from Mr. Penderby, sat down in the chair. *Am I really doing this?* she asked herself. *Will it turn me into a young lady?*

The other girls formed a half ring to watch, their faces full of excitement.

Mr. Penderby reached into a straw basket and pulled out a large red-striped sheet of cloth. With a deft movement, he flapped it in the air with a loud *fluff* and spread it over Ida so she was—other than her head—completely covered. Then he pinned the cloth back behind her neck.

Leaning forward, the barber carefully untied Ida's braids so that her brown hair fell out, reaching the small of her back. Then he held up the ribbons that Ma had used to tie Ida's hair. "Guess you won't need these anymore. Who wants to take them?"

Dot held out a hand.

Mr. Penderby stepped back and appraised Ida's head with his professional eye. Then he reached toward his table and picked up a comb and a pair of scissors. Holding the scissors in the air, as if about to attack, he opened and shut them a few times, making rapid clicking noises.

The sound was dreadful to Ida's ears. And everyone was staring at her.

Ida suddenly had a thought: *Trudy has bobbed hair, and she isn't modern.*

Mr. Penderby stepped forward to make the first cut.

Ida saw the ribbons in Dot's hand and heard her mother's voice: "Just be yourself, love."

"No," Ida said, abruptly. "I don't want to do it."

"You have to," said Lulu.

"No, I don't," returned Ida.

"Yes, no?" said the barber, looking from the girls to Ida.

"No," Ida repeated, surer of herself than ever.

With a snappy flourish, Mr. Penderby removed the sheet. "No harm done." He offered a hand as Ida stepped off the chair.

The girls reassembled outside the barbershop. Dot handed Ida her ribbons. "I'm glad you're keeping your braids," she whispered.

Ida clutched the ribbons.

"Oh well," said Helene. "It's always good to have someone different. Who's president next week?"

"I'll be," offered Lulu. "And I've got a tasty idea."

That night, Ida stood before her mirror and combed out her hair with her Christmas brush, the way Ma had so often done. Then she wove two braids. With particular care, she used her mother's ribbons to tie them off.

As she settled into bed, she was sure she heard Ma say again: "Just be yourself, love."

"I'm trying," said Ida aloud. Then she added, "But sometimes it's hard."

But I should get new ribbons, she decided. *Brighter ones.*

THIRTEEN

NEXT THURSDAY—RIGHT AFTER the last class of the day—Ida and Dot walked into room 218. It was deserted.

"Think everyone will come?" said Ida.

"Lulu will. She's the next president."

Sure enough, Lulu rushed in. "Wait till you hear my ducky idea!" she cried.

Becky and Helene arrived.

"Okay," Lulu said. "Since I'm this week's president, I decided we should all learn that swanky new dance, the Charleston. Does anyone know it?"

No one said yes.

"I don't know it either," Lulu went on. "But I want to. It's the kippiest thing in the world. Comes from a New York City Broadway show called *Runnin' Wild*."

"How do you know about it?" asked Helene.

"I have a cousin in New York City," said Lulu, "and she said that if you want to be a flapper, you absolutely must know that dance."

"What's a flapper?" asked Becky.

"A Jane that's completely free. The opposite of a dumb Dora. You know, modern."

"I'm for that," said Becky.

"Who's going to teach us?" said Helene.

"Miss Mickle. I asked her, and she told me she knew the dance and would love to teach us. She even has the music. She can come next Thursday."

"Ducky!" cried Becky.

"I always wanted to be a hoofer," said Helene.

"So, next time," said Lulu, "bring your dancing shoes."

The meeting went on with a general sharing of gossip.

"I've never done anything like dancing that Charleston," Dot confessed to Ida as they left school after the meeting.

"Neither have I," said Ida. "But I love new things."

When Ida walked into the house, she found Trudy sitting on the living room couch. There was an open scrapbook on her lap, but she wasn't looking at it. She was staring across the room, her face full of sorrow. Trudy didn't seem to notice that Ida was standing by the door.

Ida followed Trudy's gaze to the picture of Ralph Warren, the man she had been going to marry.

Not sure what to do or say, Ida remained where she was.

But Trudy must have noticed her, because she started to speak. "Today is Ralph's birthday. He was such a fine young man, Ida. So kind. Handsome. Tall. Full of energy and ideas.

"I was working here—teaching geography, believe it or not—when I met him, in 1916. He was a teller at the bank. He courted me. And . . . we had just decided to get married when America went into the war. His grandfather was in the Civil War. His father went to Cuba, fighting Spain. So, when we got into the European war, Ralph felt he had to volunteer.

"I wanted to marry him before he went, but he said it would be wiser to wait to make sure he got back. Said he didn't want me to be a merry widow. He liked to joke like that. Besides, if I married, I would lose my job. You look surprised, but I'm afraid that sort of thing happens. Remember how we talked about lady teachers being unmarried.

"He went over and fought and came out okay. It was when he got back to America that he became sick. The flu epidemic. In Camp Merritt. Somewhere in the state of New Jersey. He died there. 1920. All alone. It was terrible.

"I've read that fifty million people died in the epidemic, more than in all the war. They say it started in Kansas. I don't really know.

"Since Ralph and I hadn't married, it took me a while to learn what happened to him. I had no idea. I just thought he had changed his mind about me. Then I learned he had taken out life insurance, and all the money came to me. I considered moving to Denver. But I had a job here. It seemed wiser to stay put. And Ralph's money allowed me to buy this house. I decided that's what he would have wanted. I ordered it from Sears and Roebuck. You can see the different houses you can get in their catalog. They shipped all the parts here. Local folks put it up. That was two years ago. I miss him very much."

"I'm sorry," Ida said quietly.

"We had wanted a family," continued Trudy, as if Ida hadn't spoken. "Of course, that never happened. I'm so glad I kept my job. But I admit, I can get lonely. When I met you at your school last spring, I thought of you as the daughter Ralph and I hoped we would have. Is that a dreadful thing to confess?"

Ida shook her head. She felt Trudy's ache, but again all she could say was "I'm sorry." The words felt weak.

"You're not my daughter," said Trudy, forcing a smile. "And I promise, Ida, I won't pretend you are. But my new house felt empty. I'm so glad you're here."

"Is . . . is there some way I can help?" Ida asked.

"Just your being here brings me great joy."

"It means a lot to me, too," said Ida.

"That makes me extra happy," said Trudy. She closed the scrapbook, sat up a little straighter, and said, "Too much about me. Tell me about your day."

"The Secret Sisters had another meeting. We're going to learn a dance."

"A polite dance, I hope," Trudy said with a small smile. "And your classes?"

"They're okay."

"Are you keeping up?"

"I think so."

"Those midterm exams will come sooner than you think. Ida, they are so important."

"I know," said Ida.

"And Mr. Langly? How are things going with him?"

"I try to avoid him."

"That's wise."

"He scares me a bit," Ida admitted.

Trudy nodded. "He has a lot of power over what happens in his school." She was silent for a moment, then she shook herself and stood up. "May I give you a hug, Ida?"

"I guess . . ."

Though Ida barely lifted her arms, Trudy hugged her and said, "You're a very special person."

"Thank you," said Ida, feeling awkward as she stepped away. "Can I ask you something personal?"

"Please."

"How old are you?"

"Thirty-two."

"More than twice as old as me."

Trudy smiled. "I am."

"Are you very different than when you were my age?"

"Oh my . . . that is complicated. I suppose I'm the same person but with completely different thoughts. Sort of. I read somewhere that when you're a baby, you have new skin every month. When you're older, that still happens, though it takes longer. I was born in 1893. The world is so different now. Cars. Telephones. Airplanes. Radio. Movies. The way people dress. And act."

Ida waited as Trudy became thoughtful. "All I know," she finally said, "is that, though you can try to prevent it, everything changes. And then again, nothing seems to. It . . . it can be confusing."

"Are you going to stay in Steamboat always?"

"I have a job. I can support myself. I have friends. I have my home. A car. I don't want to lose any of that. Unfortunately, Ida, as I've indi-cated, things can be hard for unmarried women."

Not knowing what to say, Ida said nothing.

"Well," said Trudy with another small smile, "it's not something you need to think about. Not yet. Someday I'd like to show you my scrapbook. Pictures of Ralph and me."

"I'd like that."

"Just not today."

As Ida started up the steps to her room, Trudy called out, "Tomorrow night, let me take you to a movie. You said you've never seen one. *The Thief of Bagdad* is showing. People say it's wonderful. Would you like that? I would enjoy treating you."

"I'd love it."

That night, Ida kept thinking about Trudy, that man she was going to marry, and the life she was now living. It seemed such a sad story.

Ida unwound the ribbons around her braids. Trudy was thirty-two. Was that old or young? Ida tried to imagine what she would be like at that age. Would she be like Trudy? No, she wanted a life that filled more than a scrapbook. *Scrap. What an awful place in which to put your life.*

I'm being unkind, Ida scolded herself. Losing Ralph must have been terrible for Trudy. But here she was, living in this fine house only because Ralph had died. How painful. It would be like . . . like always being hugged by someone who wasn't there.

And Trudy isn't really that old.

If only, thought Ida, *she could find more hope.* She thought of that poem:

Hope is the thing with feathers—
That perches in the soul—
And sings the tune without the words—
And never stops—at all.

I must be kinder to Trudy. Appreciate what she's doing for me. And really, she is nice.

But what, Ida asked herself as she brushed her hair, *do I hope for myself?*

I'm going to be a teacher. She thought she knew what that meant. But what did she hope for in her *life*?

A great jumble of things filled Ida's head: to be liked, to do well, to be loving to her family, to her new friends, to grow.

To be taller than Ma!

All those ideas were so fuzzy they didn't seem real. Remembering what Trudy had said, she asked herself: *Am I a special person? I don't think so.*

Not like the man Trudy was going to marry.

Ida knew little about the Great War, only that it had been immense and far away. She looked across the room at the Peace Dollar. "I'm here," Ida said aloud, "because someone, a soldier I didn't know, died all alone."

How can something so good—being here in Steamboat—come from something so bad?

Slipping into her nightgown, Ida remembered that Lulu's mother had died in the epidemic too. *Did that make Lulu the person she is?*

And Dot . . . why is she so sad?

Becky, so serious, cautious, but full of life. Even though she tells us her brother is always in trouble. How does she do that?

Helene—funny and smart—but always looking messy. Why?

Why does everything and everyone suddenly have a question attached? Back home everything had an answer. It's the opposite here. Steamboat is a small town, but it's crowded with big questions.

To cheer herself up, Ida tried to recall what she knew about movies. *Pictures that move* was the best she could come up with.

A swell of emotion swept over her: *Every day I discover something I didn't know. Today I learned a lot more about Trudy. Next, the movies. Next week I'll learn that dance. I need to learn everything. Learning is wonderful. But at the same time—hard. Why is something good hard?*

Because, she told herself, *the more you learn, the more things change. It's not the learning that's hard—it's the changing. A new haircut wouldn't really have been a change. But learning about Trudy and Ralph changes me, because it makes me understand more—and ask even more questions.*

Ida snapped her fingers a few times. *At least that's getting better.*

As she began to drift off to sleep, she softly sang the words from Miss Mickle's song:

*"In the meantime, in between time
Ain't we got fun?"*

Ida's last thought of the day was: *I love all the in-betweens.*

FOURTEEN

Dear Everybody (Omnes),

I saw a movie!!

It was the most amazing thing I ever saw. Trudy (Miss Sedgewick) took me. It cost thirty cents. She treated me.

The theater is called the Orpheum. I don't know what that means. It is right on Lincoln Avenue between 8th and 9th Streets.

The building looks like an ordinary brick place, but you go inside and buy a ticket. Trudy says the space where you buy a ticket is called a foyer. (That's a French word.)

You take your ticket and go into a big, dim

room full of seats. I think fifty people were there.

The floor of the room slopes down, like the ground by our house. On the ceiling is a bunch of electric lights. In the front of the room is a big white square. In front of that square, a man was sitting at a piano.

After a while, the ceiling lights went out and the man began to play the piano. Then all of a sudden on the screen it said,

The Thief of Bagdad

(I don't know where Bagdad is.)

Next came a picture of a man dressed all in white. On the ground lay a girl—a little bit like me—looking at him. The man was stirring a pot—actually MOVING—and smoke was floating up—really floating—into a sky full of stars. Then the stars shifted and made words that said, "Happiness must be earned."

And then so many things happened, I can't tell you all of them. There was a young man who ran like a deer and climbed like a squirrel. He had a rope that you could throw straight up into the air and then climb. A white horse with wings flew through the sky. Monsters. Fire!

And that man who ran everywhere was a thief,

but he became sorry he was a thief when he fell in love with a princess who died but came back to life. Then they got married, and went away on a magic carpet that flew through the air!!!

Best of all, the magic was real because I SAW it happen. Right here in the middle of Steamboat Springs. It was the most fantastic thing in the world. Yes, I know it wasn't real, but it looked real. I wished it were real.

But I still don't know where Bagdad is. I will look it up.

And that man who played the piano did so for the whole time!

Your daughter and sister,
Ida Bidson

P.S. How is Bluebell?
P.P.S. Scratch her rump for me.
P.P.P.S. And give Shelby a kiss.
P.P.P.P.S. I looked it up. Bagdad is in the Kingdom of Iraq.
P.P.P.P.P.S. I'm not sure where that kingdom is. But guess what? Douglas Fairbanks, the handsome actor who made the movie and was the

thief, grew up in Denver, COLORADO!

Your Ida

Extra P.S. I want so much to fly on a magic carpet.
Extra, extra P.S. to Felix: You can come with me, but I'll steer. You work the brakes. Ha!!

FIFTEEN

WHEN THE SECRET SISTERS gathered for lunch each day, there seemed to be no end of things to talk about. Who did what. Had you heard this? Everybody had something to say. And share.

Lulu talked a lot about her father's friend Miss Gemelli. "She's nothing but a piffle pill. A low lid. My father wants to marry her. Ugh! If she becomes my stepmother, I'm going to take the air."

"What's that mean?" asked Ida.

"To go away," explained Dot.

"Where would you go?" Helene asked Lulu.

"The Big Apple."

"Where's that?" asked Ida.

"New York City."

"I heard that New York is full of sin," said Becky.

"That's why Lulu is going there," said Helene with a grin.

"Be the monkey's necktie," agreed Lulu happily.

Laughter.

Ida said, "You know, we shouldn't study Latin; we should study Flapper. Let Lulu be the teacher."

More laughter.

Helene talked about a second-year boy she thought was hip, but whom her father didn't like. And about the chocolate sundaes at Chamberlain's Pharmacy.

Becky said she would like a boyfriend who had lots of money, because her parents always worried about it. "I don't think I want to marry, but if I do, he has to be rich."

Dot never talked about her home but about her reading instead.

While Ida talked about becoming a teacher, she mostly listened to everyone's stories and tried to understand them. She decided that just listening to people made them feel better. As far as she could tell, that was certainly the case for Trudy.

Ida also decided that getting together with friends was the best part of her day. *I love everything about my life. I'm living in the modern world.*

And now I'm about to learn a flapper dance.

On Thursday, the Secret Sisters met in room 326 right after dismissal. The empty room was on the top floor of the school. Bars of afternoon sunlight beamed through the large windows, making the wooden floor gleam. No desks. The only thing there was a deflated basketball in a corner.

"The only time I've danced," Ida told Dot as they came in, "was square dancing at my old schoolhouse."

"I've never done any dancing," said Dot.

Becky strolled in. "What are we going to do for music?" she asked.

"Lulu said Miss Mickle has it."

All in a rush, Helene appeared. "Am I late?" she asked breathlessly. As usual, she seemed to be coming apart; one section of her hem was torn, and it dangled.

"We were just waiting for everyone to come," said Ida.

Helene sat on the floor and kicked off her shoes. "I don't have good shoes for dancing."

"What are good shoes?" asked Ida.

"Bare feet, I hope," said Becky.

"Get a wiggle on," cried Helene.

Lulu arrived. She was carrying a box, which Ida recognized as the phonograph Miss Mickle used in class. "Miss Mickle will be here in a minute," said Lulu. "She asked me to bring up her machine." She set it on the floor.

Within moments, Miss Mickle walked in. Along with the same green dress she had worn while teaching, she now also had long strings of white beads around her neck. "Hello, girls," she called, full of smiles.

There was a chorus of *hello*s in return.

"All right, girls, does your club have a name?"

"Secret Sisters," said Ida.

"I love that," said Miss Mickle. "I'll be a Sister too."

She held up what looked like a square folder. "I've brought the music. Now, what do any of you know about the Charleston?"

"It's from a Broadway show in New York City," said Lulu.

Miss Mickle nodded. "It's called *Runnin' Wild.* Isn't that something?"

"Ab-so-lute-ly," said Lulu.

"Did you see the show?" Becky asked Miss Mickle.

"I'm afraid I've never been out east."

"My cousin saw it," said Lulu. "In New York City."

"Lucky pup," said Miss Mickle.

She wound up the machine, then dropped a disc on the turntable and set it spinning.

"Now," she said, "first I'll show you the dance steps. Line up in front of me."

The five girls did as they were told.

"Just know," explained Miss Mickle, "that basically the Charleston is a seven-step dance, though of course, as you'll see, it's a lot more than that. Some silly folks actually think it's naughty. I suppose that's because when you dance it, you're free to do all kinds of wiggles and waggles. But you're the Secret Sisters, and it's 1925. So, this dance is all about freeing your body."

"Wow," murmured Becky.

To which Lulu added, "Copacetic."

Miss Mickle set the needle on the record. But before any sound started, she began to bounce on her toes while snapping her fingers. "Let's hear those snaps!" she called. "Now, follow the rhythm!"

With some success, the girls tried snapping their fingers.

The music burst forth, raucous and rhythmic, with a banjo twanging, a cornet blaring, and a piano thumping.

It brought wide smiles to the girls' faces.

Miss Mickle began to dance, stepping deftly forward and back, leaning in, arms out, moving them up and down, hands flexed, while kicking her heels back and off to the side. It was as if the music was inside her, and she was letting it spin away everywhere, while the beads around her neck tossed about wildly.

Ida decided that Miss Mickle looked like a happy, floppy scarecrow set free from its pole. Wishing she could be like that too, she tried, but hardly knew how to begin. She did snap her fingers as loudly as she could.

Lulu, meanwhile, began her own energetic

imitation of the dance.

Helene bounced up and down in place.

Dot waved her arms cautiously.

Becky did rhythmic shrugs with her shoulders.

The music soon ended, and Miss Mickle, breathless, stopped.

The girls applauded.

"Now," said Miss Mickle, "let's start by doing the seven steps without music. I'll do it, and you imitate me while I count the beat. Okay. One, two, three, four, five, six, seven. And again, one, two, three, four, five, six, seven. Good, Becky. Excellent, Lulu. Dot, throw yourself into it. Ida, come on, loosen up. There, much better. Now, the same thing with music." Miss Mickle set the needle to the record and the music blared again. "One, two, three, four, five, six, seven," she counted loudly.

With the record repeating, the Sisters tried to do the moves while watching Miss Mickle dance, even as she gave each girl suggestions.

Ida began to move with greater ease, her enthusiasm and energy growing, a big smile stretching her cheeks as she and Dot faced one another, their arms and legs flailing in all directions. Ida had never seen Dot so happy.

"I love dancing," cried Dot. "I'm going to do this for the rest of my life."

"Me, too," said Ida.

Everyone was dancing.

"What is going on here?" a voice boomed into the room.

Instantly, the dancing stopped. They all turned to see who had spoken. Standing in the doorway was the school principal. Mr. Langly was not smiling.

In haste, Miss Mickle took the needle off the record. The music ceased. She flicked a switch. The turntable stopped spinning. For a moment there was only an awful silence.

"Miss Mickle," said the principal, his voice stern, "can you please tell me *what* is going on?"

"These girls have their own club, and they asked me to provide a dance lesson."

"What kind of club? What kind of dance?"

"The Secret Sisters," said Helene.

"That new popular dance, the Charleston," said Lulu.

"And that awful music?"

"The Hoosier Radio Boys," said Miss Mickle.

Mr. Langly frowned. They all waited for him to speak. "I'm not sure this is acceptable," he finally said. "This may be what people call modern, but it's not at all ladylike." He turned to study the girls, who waited for what else he would say.

Then Ida realized he was looking at her.

"Was this your idea, Miss Bidson?"

Ida felt as if she had been smacked across the face.

Lulu, coming to Ida's defense, burst out, "Nerts, pal. What you said proves you're just an old fogie who likes sucking balloons."

Mr. Langly's face turned red. "Miss Gallagher, does your father know you're doing this? I doubt it. Shall I tell him? As for now, school has been dismissed for the day. And—your club is disbanded. No more meetings. Please go home. Miss Mickle, come to my office *now*. Miss Bidson, you will see me in my office first thing tomorrow morning." With that, Mr. Langly marched out, leaving a stunned silence behind him. No one moved.

"Oh dear," Miss Mickle finally said. "Girls, I'm terribly sorry."

"He's one big fakeloo artist," said Lulu.

"Yeah," said Helene, "everything was copacetic."

"Why did he say that to me?" asked a shaken Ida. "What's going to happen when I see him?"

"He's my father's friend," said Lulu with a scowl. "Trust me. He's nothing but a gink."

"Are you going to get in trouble?" Becky asked Miss Mickle.

"I think I already am."

"It was so much fun," said Helene.

"It was," agreed Miss Mickle. "Lulu, would you please take the phonograph machine down to my classroom?"

"Hope he doesn't tell my father," Lulu said, a note of concern entering her voice. Ida had never heard her friend sound worried before. "If I get into trouble, I could get the bum's rush out of here."

Ida turned to Miss Mickle. "Is something bad going to happen to me?" she asked.

"Ida, you've done nothing wrong."

The unhappy girls trooped down the stairs. Ida, deeply upset, trailed behind.

"Is that the end of the Secret Sisters?" asked Helene.

"Just have to be more secret," said Lulu.

"If I get into trouble, my parents will be furious," said Becky.

"I hope Miss Mickle doesn't get fired," Dot said.

"What if she does?" asked Helene.

No one had an answer.

"Can you walk me to my train?" Dot asked Ida when they headed away from the school. For a couple of blocks, neither spoke. "Dancing was so great," Dot said. "And that was so mean of Mr. Langly."

"Why did he think it was my idea?" asked Ida.

"I bet he's had it in for you since you corrected him in homeroom, remember?"

Ida stopped walking. She felt ill. "I forgot. Trudy told me he could ask me to leave school."

"Be horrible," said Dot. "I wish I could speak what I think—the way Lulu does."

"Even if we don't know what she's saying half the time," said Ida. "Do you really think Langly could kick me out?"

"Lulu said Langly and her father are friends. Bet that's how she gets away with what she does.

Langly has to say *something*, so he picks on you. People do that."

When the girls reached the railroad tracks, they stopped talking.

After a while, Ida asked, "Is it frightening on the train?"

"Was a bit, at first. I'm used to it now."

They stood silently, waiting.

"Dot, I'm scared about my meeting with Mr. Langly."

"So am I," said Dot. She was quiet for a moment, and then she said, "Ida, if he makes you leave school, I might never see you again. And you're my best friend."

"You're mine," returned Ida.

They continued to stand there. Then Dot said, "Do you think you could come home with me tomorrow night? Spend the night?"

"Might be my last day in school."

"That's why I want you to come this week. It might be our only chance."

"I'll have to ask Trudy."

"I'm sure Mr. Whitcombe—he's the engineer—will let you ride with me. Do you have a phone where you are living?"

"I think it's number one-four-five, whatever that means."

The steady clanging of a bell could be heard. Within moments, a huge black locomotive swung into view and drew slowly near, blowing dark smoke.

Some fifteen feet tall, with the brass number 302 below the smokestack, it was the biggest machine Ida had ever seen: massive iron wheels, with moving rods, tubes, and bulging parts, steam and smoke spewing and spitting like a leaky bucket. It reeked of oil and coal. To Ida, it was scary and enthralling.

"How far does it go?" she yelled over the noise.

"Denver, I guess. Or further. I get off at Oak Creek, but sometimes I think I should stay on it."

"Where would you go?"

"Told you. I wouldn't care. Long as it's far away."

The train crept along until, with squealing and screeching, it came to a halt. A man with a striped cap looked out from the high engine cab window. "How do, Miss Dot!"

"Hi, Mr. Whitcombe! This is my best friend, Ida."

"Hello there!"

Dot grabbed hold of an iron railing right next to some iron steps, climbed up, and disappeared into the cab, only to pop her head out and call down, "Ida! My father has a phone in his store. I'll call you tonight."

"I've never used a phone," Ida shouted back over the train's clamor.

"You never danced the Charleston before either," said Dot.

With its whistle blaring, its smokestack puffing and huffing, and Dot waving, the engine began to move, leaving Ida to watch it and its trail of cars roll away. A thin rain of soot drifted silently down over her.

As Ida stood there, gazing at the departing train, she thought about how Dot wanted to go away while she herself wanted to stay.

Walking slowly, she continued thinking about Mr. Langly and tomorrow's morning meeting. What if he expelled her from school?

Then a whole other thought came to her. Even if Mr. Langly didn't kick her out, what would happen when Trudy learned about the dancing? She recalled what Trudy had said: "The way people judge you and your friends reflects on me, too. I have to think of my own reputation. And protect myself. No one else will."

At the time Ida hadn't fully understood. Now she did: if what she had done was considered bad, it could be Trudy who might ask her to leave.

Sixteen

"THIS IS CORNED BEEF tomato toast à la Bradley," said Trudy, setting out dinner.

"Who's Bradley?"

"I guess the person who made it up. How was your day today?"

"Classes were good. And we had our club meeting—the Secret Sisters." Ida paused and then said, "Miss Mickle gave us a lesson about dancing the Charleston."

Trudy put down her fork and carefully patted her lips with a napkin.

"Oh yes. I'm afraid we need to talk. When I returned to school this afternoon, I learned all about it."

"What did you learn?"

"It seems Mr. Langly heard very loud, rude music coming from the top floor. When he went to investigate, he discovered you girls—and Miss Mickle—dancing wildly."

"It wasn't wild."

"He thought so."

"It was just . . . fun."

"Some people think being wild is fun."

"Mr. Langly said we can't have our club anymore."

"So I gather."

"Can he do that?"

"He is the principal, Ida."

"Is Miss Mickle in trouble?"

"Teachers need to set an example for their students."

"She's my favorite teacher."

"She's young. And inexperienced. Everyone has to learn."

"Do we have to learn not to have fun?"

"It needs to be *proper* fun. As I suggested to you when you first came, you're becoming a young lady."

"If being a young lady means I have to stop

dancing with my Secret Sisters, I don't want to become one!"

"Ida! What a thing to say. Maybe you should all join the Steamboat Women's Club. We could start up a kind of junior-miss auxiliary. There is always a need for good works."

Trudy ate in silence until Ida suddenly said, "There was something else. Mr. Langly said I had to see him first thing in the morning."

"Oh dear. I hadn't heard that."

"I'm worried he's going to tell me to leave school."

"Why would he do that?"

"He said the dance lesson was my fault."

"Was it?"

"No. And anyway, I don't think dancing is a *fault*."

"I'm afraid Mr. Langly . . . well . . . I warned you, he likes to be right."

Ida studied her uneaten dinner. Then she looked up. "The second week of classes, Mr. Langly came into our homeroom and said Governor Routt—the man the county is named after—was *Edward* Routt."

"And?"

"I told him he was wrong and gave him the right name."

"Oh my. Ida, as I also told you, that was *not* wise. Young people should not correct their elders, especially in public. As I've tried to advise you, you *must* act properly. It's not just about you. It's me, too. Since you're living with me, what you do can bring judgment on me. I've seen it. People often blame parents—or guardians—for what their young people do."

"What could happen?" cried Ida.

"I could lose friends, or, at the worst . . . my job."

"I don't want that to happen."

"I'm sure you don't. Yet, parents and guardians have a responsibility for their young. But young people forget they have a responsibility the other way, too."

Neither spoke for a few moments until Ida said, "Do you think Mr. Langly will tell me to go home?"

"He *can*."

"But . . . will he?"

Before Trudy could reply, a bell rang, startling Ida, who had no idea what it was.

"Goodness," said Trudy, standing up. "The telephone. That doesn't happen very often." She left the kitchen. Ida, curious, followed her into the living room.

Trudy was holding the telephone by its long neck with one hand, the mouthpiece near her lips, while simultaneously pressing the hearing tube to her ear with her other hand.

"Hello? Hello? Yes? This is Gertrude Sedgewick. Whom do you wish to speak to? Ida? Ida Bidson? Why, yes. Just a moment, please."

Trudy handed the telephone to Ida. "Someone is calling you," she said, puzzlement in her voice. "I don't think it's your parents."

Not sure what to do, Ida held the phone in her hands and just stood there.

"Put the receiver to your ear," Trudy coached. "Your lips to the mouthpiece. Then say hello. Loudly."

Feeling clumsy, Ida struggled to do as told. "Hello," she said.

"Louder," urged Trudy.

"Hello!" Ida shouted.

In return, she heard a rough, hollow voice say "Ida?"

"Yes."

"It's me, Dot."

Ida looked at the receiver as if Dot were inside the telephone.

"Who is it?" asked Trudy.

"My best friend, Dot."

"That's fine. You can speak to her."

"Dot?"

"Ida, my mother said you can visit tomorrow night and stay over. Can you?"

"I'll have to ask." To Trudy, Ida said, "My friend wants me to visit with her from after school tomorrow till Saturday."

"Goodness! Is that your Oak Creek friend?"

Ida nodded.

"How will you even get there? And back?"

"The train."

"What about your studies?"

"I'll have the rest of the weekend."

"I have to think about this. Ask if you can call back. Get her number."

"Dot, I'll call back. What's your number?"

"One-two-four-six."

Ida hung up and waited for Trudy to speak.

"Ida, I don't know anything about these people."

"Dot's my best friend."

"But Oak Creek . . . and she wants you to travel by train."

"She does it every day. Twice a day."

"I'm not sure what to say," said Trudy. She sat very still, her hands clasped. "I do wonder about where they're from."

"Oak Creek."

"No, I mean before they got there. I wish I could speak to your mother."

"Can I tell you what my ma once said to me?" asked Ida. "I always try to remember it."

"Of course."

"I had just met someone, and I told Ma I didn't like her. She said, 'You've watched me make bread. First you mix it and knead it, but then you have to wait till it rises. That's how you get good bread. Ida, it's the same with friends. Takes time.'"

Trudy, staring into her hands, was silent for a long while.

"Tomorrow," said Ida, "might be my last day in Steamboat. I might never ever see Dot again."

"Of course you will," said Trudy, sounding frustrated. "But you must promise to study extra hard when you get back."

"I will."

"Let me call Dot's mother. What's her last name?"

"Kovács."

Trudy hesitated, then picked up the phone. "Give me her number."

"One-two-four-six."

After another long moment, Trudy clicked the receiver holder a few times and said, "Gertrude Sedgewick here. Can you connect me with one-two-four-six?"

A nervous Ida kept her eyes on Trudy.

"Hello. Mrs. Kovács? This is Miss Sedgewick. In Steamboat. Your daughter—a classmate of my boarder, Ida Bidson—has invited Ida to visit tomorrow night. In Oak Creek. Is that right?"

Ida stood by, listening.

"Well, thank you. I'd be happy to drive them. Oh, well, are you sure it's safe? Glad to hear it. I'm sure she will enjoy that. Thank you. Good night." She handed the phone back to Ida. "Your friend has something to say."

Ida took the phone. "Dot?" she said.

Dot said, "Good luck tomorrow, Ida. Be brave."

Ida hung the receiver on the hook and set the phone down.

"Well, that should be interesting," Trudy said to Ida, though her voice suggested she thought otherwise. "A visit with your new friend. I offered to drive you, but as you said, Dot wants you to take the train with her. Mrs. Kovács says it's perfectly safe. Have you ever ridden on a train?"

Ida shook her head.

"And in the engine cab," said Trudy, sounding worried.

"The engineer is her friend."

"Well, then. There you are. I suppose you can. She said you could come back by train Saturday morning. I just hope I'm doing the right thing by letting you go."

Trudy took a deep breath and then returned her attention to Ida. "Now, we were talking about that meeting tomorrow with Mr. Langly. My advice, dear, is just apologize."

"For what?"

"Whatever he says you did."

"But I didn't do anything."

"Ida, things will go better if you do as I

suggest. People in positions of authority like to hear apologies."

"The dancing was Lulu's idea," Ida blurted out. "But Mr. Langly is a friend of Lulu's father. So, he picked me out, because I told him he was wrong about something. He's just a fakeloo artist. It's not fair!"

"You may be right," said Trudy, "but as you have seen, being right doesn't necessarily help when it comes to people like Mr. Langly. And since I said you could go to Oak Creek, perhaps you could take my advice about him."

"It's not the same," cried Ida.

"Now, Ida—"

"I don't want to make things bad for you!"

"Ida, please, tell Mr. Langly the truth—that the dancing was Lulu's idea—apologize for taking part, and then say you won't do anything like that again. And do find something nice to say to him."

"I hate this," cried Ida, and with that, she raced up to her room, slammed the door behind her, and threw herself on her bed. *I'm not going to apologize for something I didn't do, and anyway, it wasn't wrong.*

There was a tap on her door.

"I'm in bed," Ida called.

Trudy went away.

Ida kept telling herself that she didn't want to get Lulu in trouble. Or make problems for Trudy. Or accept Mr. Langly's notion that having fun with the Secret Sisters was being wild.

Except both Trudy and Mr. Langly thought it was. And the dancing *had* been Lulu's idea.

Ida didn't know what to do. Should she tell him Lulu had suggested the dancing? Should she apologize? But if so, for what? The only thing she was sure of was that tomorrow might be her last day of high school.

She thought about her new life. All the learning she was doing. Her new friends. Even her talks with Trudy. She loved it all. To lose it would be a catastrophe. She had thought going to high school would be so simple. She'd just go. Become a teacher. And it all turned out to be so complicated. But she still loved it!

Into her mind came Ma's words: "Just be yourself." Even that wasn't as simple as Ida had once supposed. What did being herself even mean now?

Ida, trying to decide what she was and what

she would do in the morning, lay very still.

Suddenly, she realized something: she had actually used a telephone. She had spoken to Dot, who was twenty miles away!

Her new world was amazing. Or it would be if she could get through the next day . . .

SEVENTEEN

⁓

It was a tense Ida who, as she stepped into school, found Lulu waiting for her just beyond the door.

"Are you going to tell Langly the dancing was my idea?" Lulu instantly asked.

"I—"

Lulu interrupted. "Listen. I never told you. I got kicked out of my Craig school. Only Langly and my father are friends, so Langly said I could come here, to his school. That's why we moved. The thing is, my old man warned me that if I got thrown out of this place, he'd send me to a boarding school, a strict one. If he does, I'll die. So, if Langly tells my father that I . . ."

"Why were you kicked out?"

"Got caught smoking a cigar in school."

"A cigar!" In spite of everything, Ida had to laugh.

"Someone dared me. It was a setup. I know. I was a ripe rube. Are you going to tell Langly?"

"Well, I was going—"

"Airtight!" cried Lulu, and, without letting Ida say another word, ran off.

Ida, watching her go, thought, *Lulu's always trying to be shocking. But she isn't, not really. At least not to us. Mr. Langly might feel differently, though.*

When Ida walked into the office, Miss Ogden was at her desk. "Hello, Ida," she said. "Here for your meeting with Mr. Langly?"

"Yes, ma'am."

"I'll tell him you're here," returned Miss Ogden with a look that suggested she knew all about what was happening. She went through the rear door and shut it behind her.

The office had a couple of high-backed wooden chairs, so Ida sat down and looked around. There was Miss Ogden's desk. There were three wooden file cabinets against one wall. On another wall was a framed map. Across the top, it read "Colorado."

Restless, Ida studied it. It took her a few seconds to find "Steamboat Springs" printed in small letters. "Denver" was in big, bold letters. Seeing it made Ida wonder how her friend Tom was doing. What would he make of the fact that she was in trouble? She tried to imagine him doing the Charleston. The thought made her smile.

She searched for Elk Valley on the map. It wasn't on this one, either.

Ida was still gazing at the map when Miss Ogden returned. "Mr. Langly will see you now." She stood by the open door and let Ida pass. As Ida glanced up at her, Miss Ogden averted her eyes.

I'm definitely in big trouble, thought Ida.

Mr. Langly was sitting behind a large desk, bent over some papers, reading. To one side of his desk lay his old German shepherd. Though Ida stood right before Mr. Langly, he appeared not to notice she was there.

But as the principal continued to read, the dog heaved himself up and, with a slowly wagging tail, came over to where Ida stood. She reached out and scratched one of his ears. The dog licked her hand, then returned to where he had been lying, plopped down, and rested his head on a paw. He kept his big brown eyes on Ida.

Not knowing what else to do, Ida continued to stand where she was. Mr. Langly kept reading.

He's making me wait, she thought. *Trying to scare me. But his dog likes me. And I like his dog.*

She remembered Dot's words: "Be brave." She recalled Lulu's words about the principal "sucking balloons."

Mr. Langly turned over a page and finally looked up. His thin face was severe, without the hint of a smile.

Ida, trying not to fidget, wondered how old he was and if he found his high starched collar irritating.

Mr. Langly removed his glasses and, with a small black cloth, polished the lenses, then put them on again. They made his eyes bigger.

His dog has nicer eyes, Ida thought.

"Miss Bidson," he said at last. "Thank you for coming."

"Yes, sir."

"Now, Miss Bidson, your home is up in North Routt, and you're boarding in town with Miss Sedgewick. This is your first year at Steamboat High. Previously you went to that tiny one-room school up there."

"Yes, sir," Ida replied, thinking, *He's telling me I don't belong here. But I do.*

"As I hope you've learned, down here we take education seriously. It's not futile. Do you follow me?"

"'Futile' is a Latin word. It means 'in vain.' And—"

Langly cut her off. "Now, Miss Bidson, as I understand it, that . . . group . . . of girls dancing was some sort of club. Is that correct?"

"Yes, sir."

"And you call yourselves . . . ?"

"The Secret Sisters."

Mr. Langly glowered. "Why secret?"

Ida shrugged. "Just a name."

"Who suggested it?"

"I guess I did."

"Again, why secret? Were you intending to hide what you were doing?"

"No, sir. It was just for . . . fun."

164

"Is your idea of fun wild dancing?"

Ida didn't know what to say.

"I repeat," said Mr. Langly, "is your idea of fun wild dancing?"

"I . . . don't think it was wild."

"It was," said Mr. Langly with certainty. "Whose idea was it to dance?"

As Ida stared into Mr. Langly's stern face, she thought of Lulu, but she said nothing.

"Was it Miss Mickle's?"

"No, sir."

"Well, then who? One of you girls? You?"

Ida, tense, stood without speaking, and in the heat of his glare, she knew she would be true to the Secret Sisters and to what she thought was right.

"I suspect," said Mr. Langly, "it *was* you."

Ida shook her head.

"Then who?"

"I don't want to say."

"Why?"

"Because . . . because there wasn't anything wrong with what we were doing."

Langly steepled his hands and studied Ida without speaking.

Ida, standing very still, thought, *Is he going to expel me?* She felt ill.

"I believe," said Mr. Langly, "it *was* you who suggested it."

"It wasn't."

"Then, once again, who?"

"I . . . I don't want to say."

"Why?"

"You'll . . . get them in trouble."

"I might," agreed Mr. Langly after a long moment. "I might indeed. Because I do *not* intend to let such wildness happen in my school. Furthermore, Miss Bidson, since I believe it *was* you who suggested the dance, you need to know it is within my authority to expel you from school. Permanently. Right now. Not just for unruly behavior, but for your insolence. Like correcting me in class. Punishing you would set an example for your friends."

Ida, trembling, struggled for words. "Principal Langly . . ."

"Yes?"

"I . . . I didn't do anything wrong."

"But you did. And I won't have it." He stared at her in stony silence.

Hands clenched, Ida said, "Are . . . are you going to . . . expel me?"

"You are boarding with Miss Sedgewick, whom I greatly respect. I shall talk to her. As she is responsible for you, it is for her to ensure that you behave properly. Because if she can't control you . . .

"Of course," said Mr. Langly, "you could help yourself—and your friends—by recognizing the seriousness of your actions and apologizing."

He folded his hands, waiting for her to speak.

"I didn't . . . do anything wrong," Ida said again.

Mr. Langly made a loud sigh. "Very well, consider yourself warned. *One* more act of bad behavior, Miss Bidson—*one*—and you will be expelled."

With that, the principal picked up one of his papers and began to read it again, holding it before his face. "Dismissed," he said.

It took Ida a moment to realize she had been told to leave the room. That was when she remembered Trudy telling her to say something nice.

"Can I add one thing?" she asked.

When Mr. Langly made no reply, Ida said, "Your dog is nice." Then she spun about and left the office. The phrase "you will be expelled" kept echoing in her head.

In the outside office, Miss Ogden was holding out a paper. "Homeroom late slip," she said.

As Ida took it, Miss Ogden leaned forward and whispered, "I heard all that. That's the way he is." Then she added: "You're a brave girl."

"Thank you," Ida managed to say.

She went out into the empty hall and stood there for a moment, wondering if she'd be expelled. *He really would do it.* Wiping a tear from her cheek, she walked slowly to homeroom. When she entered, the whole class looked at her.

Everyone knows about the dancing, thought Ida.

She handed the late slip to Miss Blake.

Quietly, the teacher said, "Are you all right?"

Ida, thinking, *She knows too,* gave a quick nod and sat down in the back row next to Dot.

"What happened?" Dot whispered.

"He said the dancing was my idea, and if I do one more bad thing, he'll expel me."

"I hate him," said Dot.

As the two girls headed for their first class,

Lulu suddenly appeared in the hallway. "Did you tell?" she asked.

When Ida shook her head, Lulu gave her a hug. "You are absolutely fish fingers!" She ran off.

But as Ida watched her go, she again heard Mr. Langly's words: "You will be expelled."

EIGHTEEN

DURING ALGEBRA, MISS MICKLE was unusually restrained, saying nothing about the day
before.

Watching her, Ida wondered what had happened when the teacher met with Mr. Langly, but
she didn't think she should ask. Then, as the class
ended, Miss Mickle called, "Miss Bidson, would
you please stay a moment?"

"I'll wait for you," whispered Dot as the students filed out.

When Miss Mickle and Ida were alone in
the room, the teacher said, "Ida, did you see Mr.
Langly this morning?"

Ida nodded.

"May I ask you what he said?"

Ida told her what happened.

"It's quite unfair," said the teacher. "And wasn't the dance lesson Lulu's idea?"

Ida nodded again.

"But you didn't tell him that?"

"She asked me not to."

"You're a good Sister," said Miss Mickle. "But I'm so very sorry."

"He told me I had to apologize," said Ida. "Do you think I should?"

"Not at all."

Ida said, "Did . . . did you meet with Mr. Langly?"

"Yes."

"What did he say to you?"

"Sort of the same as to you."

"Is he going to expel you?"

"He might fire me. But, Ida, try not to worry. Mr. Langly likes to scare people. Makes him feel good about himself." She finally smiled. "Full of horsefeathers. Now, you better get on to your class."

Ida stood there. "Aren't you worried?" she asked.

"I'm trying not to be."

"The lady I'm boarding with told me what we did was wrong. She might ask me to leave."

"Oh, Ida, that would be so unfair. That's Miss Sedgewick, isn't it? Would it help if I spoke to her?"

Ida, sensing that Trudy didn't approve of Miss Mickle, shook her head.

"Well, you're due at your next class."

Dot was waiting in the hall. "What did Miss Mickle say?"

Ida told her.

"I guess we shouldn't have danced," said Dot.

"But we loved it, and it wasn't wrong," insisted Ida.

As they hurried to class, a girl Ida didn't know stopped them in the hall and said, "Were you at that dance party with Miss Mickle?"

"Wasn't a party. But . . . sort of."

"Airtight!" exclaimed the girl, and she rushed away.

Before Ida and Dot reached class, three more students complimented them.

"We're the most famous girls in the school," said Ida.

"Don't want to be," said Dot.

When the Secret Sisters met for lunch in an

empty classroom, they all wanted to know what had happened at Ida's meeting with Langly.

Ida glanced at Lulu and then said, "He warned me that if I did something like that again, I will be expelled."

"Expelled!" cried Helene.

"If you did something like what again?" asked Becky.

"Dancing in school."

"What a flat tire," said Lulu.

Everyone laughed.

"Anyone know what Mr. Langly said to Miss Mickle?" asked Dot.

"He warned her, too," said Ida.

"Is he going to fire her?" asked Becky.

"Maybe," said Ida.

"If he does, we'll go on strike and demand she be taken back," said Lulu.

Becky said, "My father says strikes are only done by red agitators and anarchists."

"What are they?" asked Ida.

"Bad people," explained Helene. "They want to get rid of the government. By throwing bombs."

"Then I'm going to be an anarchist," Lulu announced.

"Throwing bombs?" cried Becky in horror.

"No, dancing the Charleston," Lulu said.

More laughter.

With no more talk about what happened, Ida relaxed.

But as she and Dot were leaving school at the end of the day, Mr. Langly was standing by the doorway. It was something the principal did every Friday afternoon.

"Have a nice weekend, Emily," he said to one student. "Don't forget to study this weekend, Dan," he said to another.

As Dot and Ida passed him, he said, "Enjoy your time in Oak Creek, you two."

That he knew where she was going—Trudy must have told him—annoyed Ida and made her stop. "Mr. Langly, sir, may I say something?"

"About my dog, Miss Bidson?"

Ida had wanted to say something nice about Miss Mickle but now held back, sure it wouldn't help. She was sorry she had stopped.

"It's wise to learn from your mistakes, Miss Bidson," said Mr. Langly, "as I'm sure Dorothy can tell you. Now, you girls have a nice time." He turned away from Ida and spoke to another student. "Hello, Martha. Ready for the weekend?"

As Dot and Ida walked toward the train, Dot was unusually quiet. Ida could tell she was upset, but all Ida said was "I wanted to say something to Langly, but I was afraid to. I hate being afraid. Don't you?"

Dot's reply was "How did he learn you were going to visit Oak Creek with me?"

"Trudy, probably."

Dot said nothing.

Then Ida asked, "What did Mr. Langly mean when he said you could tell me about mistakes?"

When Dot only shook her head, Ida decided not to ask more.

They walked on. "I'm so glad you're coming," said Dot.

"Me, too."

"You don't know how important it is to me. You're the best friend I ever had. But I need you to see my family."

"Why?"

"Just so you know."

"Know what?"

"If you . . . if you still want to be my friend."

"What are you talking about? Of course I'll be your friend. Why would you say that?"

"You'll see" was all Dot replied.

They reached the railway tracks, and it wasn't long before the locomotive came into view. For Ida, awed again by its size and noise, the awareness that she was actually going to get on it was exhilarating. And it seemed even more extraordinary when the gigantic engine, looming high, came to a grinding, squealing stop right in front of them.

Mr. Whitcombe, the engineer, leaned out the cab window. "Howdy, Miss Dot! Ready to head home?"

"Hi, Mr. Whitcombe. This is my friend Ida. She's coming with me."

"Is she? All right then, Miss Ida, all aboard."

Closely followed by Dot and helped by the iron railing, Ida clambered up the engine steps and into the cab. Once there, she was confronted by a wall of dials, gauges, valves, and levers. Below these mechanical things was a gaping hole through which Ida could see a blazing red fire. She stood a few feet from it and could feel the heat. It was all marvelous.

"Make yourself at home," Mr. Whitcombe called over to Ida. He was sitting on a tall stool on one side of the cab, his gloved hands on a couple of levers.

There was another man there, rather small, his overalls and face covered with soot. In his hands was a shovel.

"Hello, Mr. Eiger," Dot said to him. "This is Ida."

"How do," came Mr. Eiger's reply as he turned and dug his shovel into a pile of coal that was tumbling into the cab from the coal box. As Ida watched, he pitched the coal into the open fire hole.

Mr. Whitcombe reached up and pulled down on a cord. A whistle shrieked. The next moment, the train gave a lurch, followed by multiple clunks. Ida realized they had begun to move.

Dot beckoned Ida to the other side of the cab, where there was an open window. "You can watch," she shouted over the engine's chaotic noise.

Ida looked out and realized the speed at which they were going was faster than a car, faster than she had ever moved before. Elated, she grabbed an iron handle and clung to it. Steamboat was quickly left behind as they zipped past trees and shrubbery and moved into a gorge.

"She's never been on a train before," Dot shouted to Mr. Whitcombe.

The engineer grinned. "Welcome to the modern world, miss."

Ida gazed at the multicolored canyon walls and the fast-flowing creek that lay below. Now and again, she turned to watch Mr. Whitcombe check some of the gauges and valves. She'd never seen anything like it before. It was enthralling.

"Do you like this?" cried Dot.

"I love being modern!" Ida hollered back.

Very soon they came onto a level area. "Oak Creek!" cried Mr. Whitcombe. The whistle screamed and the bell clanged.

Ida shouted, "Can't wait to meet your family! They must be nice."

Dot made no reply, leaving Ida to again puzzle over what her friend was *not* telling her. She thought of Dot saying that Ida might not want to be friends after visiting. That was ridiculous. *Still, something isn't right,* Ida told herself.

When the train squealed to a stop, the girls climbed down from the engine cab. Once they were on the ground, the whistle howled, and the locomotive began to creep away, chuff-chuffing as it disappeared down the tracks.

"What did you think of that?" asked Dot.

"It was the tiger's spots," returned Ida. "I suppose the only thing better would be to fly in an airplane. Would you do that?"

"Don't think so."

"I would," said Ida. "You know what? I love machines."

On the other side of the train tracks was a row of houses, made of both brick and wood. "We live right over there," said Dot, pointing across the wide street. "Above the grocery store."

Ida saw a crude sign on a building: Kovács's Grocery.

Dot dropped her arm and looked down. As she led the way slowly, almost reluctantly, Ida wondered if it had been a mistake to come.

Kovács's Grocery was a scruffy wooden building fronted by a large, dirty window. Behind the glass were a couple of cereal boxes, Corn Flakes and Shredded Krumbles. Also, a few bags labeled "Oats" and "Flour," plus jars of pickles and sauerkraut. There were some canned vegetables as well as a few bottles of Nehi soda and Coca-Cola. It had a sparse look.

Just as they approached the front door, Dot stopped.

Ida had never seen her friend so tense. "What's wrong?"

"Nothing."

Dot opened the door. A bell jangled harshly. "Welcome to my home," she said, and the two girls walked inside.

NINETEEN

TO IDA, THE ROOM they stepped into seemed shabby; nothing looked new or particularly clean. One dangling electric bulb revealed three rows of shelving, two against the walls, one running down the middle. The shelves were only partially filled with boxes and cans, as if shoppers had already taken most of the goods. Or had never come.

At the front of the room, by the door, was a high counter upon which sat a metal cashbox and a telephone. On the floor in front of the counter were three open barrels, which held dried beans, rice, and oats.

Behind the counter, a man was sitting. Near him, a pair of wooden crutches leaned against the wall. Before him lay a newspaper.

The man was barrel-chested, with a rather large head and a great shock of white hair. His wrinkled face was broad, with deep-set eyes under shaggy eyebrows. He needed a shave. Ida guessed the man was Dot's father, Mr. Kovács.

When Dot came in, he looked up and gave a tight smile. "Hi there, Miss Dot. How'd your day go?"

"Fine," she returned. "Dad, this is Ida, my Steamboat High friend. Mom said I could invite her over."

"Hello," said Ida.

"You're most welcome. You live in Steamboat?"

"I board there. I'm from North Routt."

"That's a long way."

"Is everyone home?" asked Dot.

"Not sure if Jimmy is," said Mr. Kovács. "Go on up."

"This way," Dot said to Ida, and led her to some narrow steps at the back of the store.

"Who's Jimmy?"

"My younger brother."

Ida, thinking of the crutches, said in a low voice, "Did something happen to your father?"

"Mine accident," Dot whispered.

At the top of the stairs, the girls stepped into a large room, in the center of which sat a table with chairs around it. To Ida's eyes, the room was dark and dreary. Even the two windows were dirty.

"Hello," Dot called. "We're here."

An older-looking woman stepped out of a small kitchen. She seemed frail and wore a faded yellow dress that hung loosely from her narrow shoulders like an empty sleeve. Her pale face was pinched. Dull red hair streaked with gray lay about her shoulders. There was an air of weariness about her but enough resemblance to Dot for Ida to guess she was her friend's mother, Mrs. Kovács.

"Hello," the woman said, making a small gesture with her hand.

"Mom, this is Ida. I told you all about her."

The woman nervously rubbed one hand with the other, offered a small smile, and said, "I'm so glad Dot has a friend."

"Thank you," returned Ida, trying to make sense of things.

"We'll have dinner soon as Jimmy gets back

from doing his papers," said Mrs. Kovács. "Dot, why don't you show your friend your room?"

"Can I help with anything?" Dot asked.

"All done," said Mrs. Kovács.

"Come on," said Dot, tugging on Ida's sleeve. She led the way down a short hall and opened the door at the end. "Outhouse is in the backyard," she murmured.

They stepped into a small room, smaller than Ida's in Trudy's house. There was a bed, a narrow bureau, and a little bookcase stuffed every which way with scruffy-looking books.

"Kind of tight," said Dot apologetically.

"It's fine," returned Ida.

"Is your home up in North Routt bigger?"

"Sort of," said Ida, not wanting to say how much nicer it was.

Dot sat on her bed, clasped her hands, and was still. A tear rolled down her cheek.

"What's the matter?" Ida asked.

"I shouldn't have invited you," said Dot.

"Why?" Ida sat down close to her. "What's going on, Dot?"

"Everyone here tries to be happy, but they aren't. Because of what I did."

"What did you do?"

It was a long moment before Dot—not looking at Ida—began to speak. "My father worked in the Twentymile Mine. It's close to town, so a lot of men work there. My father and his brother started when they were young. Thirteen, I think.

"One day—two years ago—I wasn't at school and noticed my father had left his lunch pail behind. I took it to him. Only a lot of miners think that if girls or women go into a mine, it brings terrible luck. And . . . and it's even worse if they have red hair. I didn't know."

Ida kept her eyes on Dot's sad face.

It took a few moments for Dot to speak again. "The week after I went, there was an awful accident. It was terrible. My father's brother was killed. My father was crippled and . . . But the thing is . . . I was blamed. People said my going there made it happen.

"Since then, no one will have anything to do with me. Nothing. They think I bring . . . bad luck."

"That's terrible!" said an astonished Ida. "Do your parents believe it too?"

Dot shook her head. "No. But at school, no one would talk to me. Friends stopped being friends. Teachers wouldn't call on me. People around town aren't nice to my parents. They treat my brother badly. When I walk around town and people see me, they cross the street. The thing is, Oak Creek is full of miners, and a lot of them believe those things."

"Oh, Dot . . . how awful."

"My dad had saved a little money, so he opened this store. He doesn't have to move around much. Some people come in. Not a lot. We just get by. So, we're poor because of what I did. And that's why I go to school in Steamboat. I don't want to go here."

"Do people really think that you . . . ?"

Dot nodded.

"But that's just . . . stupid."

"My parents don't believe it," said Dot. "We talk about moving, or my boarding—like you do—but we don't have the money. When I found a way to get to Steamboat High—the train—my parents said I should go.

"My family would be better off if I weren't here. I want so badly to get away, but I can't leave with no place to go. My mother agrees. If I can get through high school, I might be able to earn enough to live someplace else.

"The best thing has been getting to know you.

You're so happy. Sweet. And smart. And the Secret Sisters. They make me happy too. Even Lulu. But . . . I was afraid to tell you what took place. That . . . that if you learned, you'd stop being my friend. I mean, maybe what happened with that dancing . . . Maybe it *was* me who got you and Miss Mickle in trouble. Maybe I am bad luck."

"It had nothing to do with you," cried Ida.

Dot smeared away another tear. "That's why I invited you here. I just wanted you to know. See how we live. You don't have to come again. Are you going to hate me?"

"I won't ever, ever stop being your friend," said Ida. "I mean, you're my best friend in the whole world."

There was a knock on the door. A woman's voice called, "Dinner!"

Dot snatched up a gray pillow, wiped her face clear of tears, and led the way out of the room.

A redheaded boy—younger than Dot—was sitting at the table.

"This is Jimmy," said Dot. "My brother."

Right away Jimmy said, "Dot told me you drove a car to your school up in North Routt. That true?"

"Yes."

"Wow!"

Ida and Dot sat down.

Mrs. Kovács went to the top of the steps. "Dinner," she shouted down. Everyone waited. Presently, Ida heard a *thump, thump*, which seemed to be ascending the stairs. *Thump, thump.*

Mr. Kovács, crutches tucked under his arms, appeared out of the stairwell. He crossed the room slowly, took hold of the back of a chair, and let the crutches drop with a crash. Then he sat down. "Did it," he said, and made the effort to smile.

Mrs. Kovács brought in plates of food, each of which held a piece of browned meat, potatoes, and bread.

Mr. Kovács turned to Ida. "What's your father do?" he asked.

"Raises sheep."

"A rancher. Good clean work."

Ida nodded.

There was not a lot of talk during dinner. Mostly, it was Jimmy asking about Ida's ranch and the animals that lived there.

When plates were empty, Dot stood up, fetched her father's crutches, and held them erect. Mr. Kovács hauled himself up, tucked the crutches under his arms, and went to the top of the steps. Just before going down, he turned to Ida. "Sometimes people come to the store late."

Dot and Jimmy cleared away the dishes. Then Dot led Ida back into her room.

Dot said, "We don't always eat good like that. That was special, for you." She sat down on the bed. "The day after I finish high school, I'll be on the train to go away as far as I can."

"But where?" said Ida.

"Where people won't know me. Or what I did."

When they went to sleep, they shared the bed, Ida holding her friend's hand tightly.

Lying in the dark, Ida thought about Dot and what people believed about her. It was such a horrible, ancient way of thinking. Then she thought of her train ride, the most modern thing ever. How could a locomotive—so modern—and believing in curses be in the same world?

She also thought about her morning meeting with Mr. Langly. Ida was sure he would tell Trudy about his threat to expel her.

As she lay there, clutching Dot's hand, Ida wondered how Trudy, who was always concerned with the proper thing, would react to Dot's story.

But Ida was glad she hadn't apologized for doing something she didn't think was wrong. The Charleston was no more wrong than Dot bringing her father lunch had been wrong. She was glad she was Dot's friend. Glad, too, she'd said nothing about Lulu.

And Ida's last thought of the day was *I'm glad I'm me.*

TWENTY

IN THE MORNING, Dot walked Ida to the train tracks.

"What'll you do all day?" Ida asked.

"Help my mother in the house, then go to the creek and read. I have a favorite spot. No one bothers me there."

"Won't you be cold?"

"I'll take a blanket."

"What are you going to read?"

"*Little Women.* I've read it so many times. I like to pretend my world is like that. Have you read it?"

"You told me about it."

"It's the best book ever. You should read it. The sisters in the book are like the Secret Sisters. Except they really are sisters."

They heard the bell of the approaching train. Dot said, "Are you sure you don't think I'm bad luck?"

"Positive," Ida said.

They hugged. "Bless you for coming," said Dot. Then she said, "Langly can't expel you."

"'Hope,'" Ida returned, "'is a thing with feathers.'"

"Or," said Dot, "a train that takes you away."

Once in the engine cab, Ida leaned out the window. "Goodbye! I love you! See you Monday."

Dot waved. She looked so sad.

As the train began to move, Mr. Whitcombe turned to Ida. "Have a good time?" he shouted.

"Yes," Ida felt compelled to say, even as she thought, *I never did tell Dot what Trudy said about Oak Creek. Or having bad friends.* She considered Trudy's fears and Dot's situation. *I'm so lucky to have my family.*

Her next thought was *But if I'm expelled, I'll be home milking Bluebell. Forever.*

It wasn't long before the train came to a halt. "Here you are, miss," said Mr. Whitcombe. "Steamboat Springs."

As soon as Ida climbed down, the train pulled away. For a moment, she stood by the tracks and watched as it vanished around a bend, trailing smoke. As she gazed after it, she again thought about unhappy Dot. *Believing Dot caused that accident is like Mr. Langly believing I suggested the dance. Why do people want to believe untrue things?*

She turned and started for home, dreading meeting with Trudy.

When she came down Lincoln Avenue and passed Sixth Street, she realized she was going by the two-story wooden building that was the town library. Wanting to delay her return to Oak Street, she went in.

The library was one large room, with three long shelves holding books. Very few of them were new, but Ida had never seen so many books before. There were also some chairs and a table.

"Yes, dear, can I help you?"

A woman was sitting at a desk. She looked perfectly nice and was smiling. Ida guessed she was somewhat older than Trudy. She had a round, welcoming face.

Ida approached her.

"Yes, miss," said Ida. "My name is Ida Bidson, and I've recently come to town. Boarding with Gertrude Sedgewick. I'm going to the high school."

"Oh yes," said the woman. "I'm Mrs. Molly, the librarian. Trudy has told me all about you. She feels so blessed to have you stay with her. She says you're an angel. Did you want to borrow a book?"

"Does . . . does it cost anything?"

"Absolutely free. But if you borrow a book and don't bring it back in time—two weeks—I'm required to fine you two cents a day. Were you interested in something particular?"

"Please," said Ida, "is there a book here called *Little Women*?"

"We have a couple of copies," said the librarian. "One of them should be available. Let's have a look."

Ida followed Mrs. Molly until she stopped and plucked a book from a shelf. She handed it to Ida. "There you are."

Ida took the thick book into her hands and opened it.

Little Women
Or
Meg, Jo, Beth, and Amy

"May I read it?"

"Every girl should."

Ida sat down at the table and began to read the first page:

"Christmas won't be Christmas without any presents," grumbled Jo, lying on the rug.

"It's so dreadful to be poor!" sighed Meg, looking down at her old dress.

"I don't think it's fair for some girls to have plenty of pretty things, and other girls nothing at all," added little Amy, with an injured sniff.

"We've got Father and Mother, and each other," said Beth.

Ida kept reading. And reading. The mother character—Marmee—was so good. The father was off at some war. What war? Ida had no idea. The book didn't say. As for the March sisters— Meg, Jo, Beth, and Amy—she adored them. Her favorite was Jo. She would like to be like Jo. So full of energy and spunk. *Wild*, in her loving way.

Ida kept reading, losing her worries in the sisters' adventures.

Two hours later she felt a tap on her shoulder. "Miss Ida," said Mrs. Molly. "I'm afraid we're about to close. But, if you'd like, you can borrow that book."

"I can?"

"Of course. Just bring it over here."

Ida carried *Little Women* to the desk. From the back of the book, Mrs. Molly pulled out a card. "Just write your name there," she said, pointing to a line on the card below many other signatures. Among them, Ida saw Dot's name three times.

Ida added her name.

Mrs. Molly put in a date. "That's when you need to bring it back. But you can renew it."

"Thank you," said Ida.

"Thanks for coming by," called Mrs. Molly as Ida walked away, clutching the book. "Say hello to Trudy for me."

When Ida reached home, Trudy was having tea and chatting with two white-haired ladies in the living room. Trudy introduced Ida to them. "Did you have a nice time with your friend?"

"Yes, thank you. On the way home I stopped at the library."

"Good for you."

"Mrs. Molly says hello. And I borrowed a book."

"Excellent. Would you like some tea?"

"I think I'll go to my room and read."

"Don't forget your studies," said Trudy. Giving Ida a knowing look, she added, "We'll talk later."

That evening, during dinner, Trudy said, "Mr. Langly spoke to me about his meeting with you yesterday."

"What did he say?"

"That you refused to apologize."

"Because I didn't do anything wrong."

"Ida, that doesn't matter. It's what he wants. He's a proud man."

"He's wrong," said Ida. "The same way he was wrong about Governor Routt's name. If someone says something that's wrong but insists it's right, does that mean he *is* right?"

"I did get him to promise he won't do anything until he sees how you do on the November exams. I also told him how good and nice you

197

are. But at the least, Ida, I urge you to keep away from those Secret Sisters of yours."

"But I love them, and we need each other!" cried Ida.

"How do you need each other?" asked Trudy.

"We help each other. We share things. We talk." Then Ida told Trudy all about Dot and what had happened to her. "How could people ever believe she caused an accident by bringing lunch to her father?"

"I can't explain it. People are supposed to be smarter. But what I've learned is, if they can't have a reason, they make up something *un*reasonable."

"Just like Mr. Langly," said Ida.

Trudy sighed. Then she said, "Dot must be lonely."

"If I'm expelled from school," said Ida, "you should invite her here to live with you."

"Let's hope you are not expelled."

"Are you going to tell me to leave?"

"I don't want to. But Ida, dear, as I've told you, I have my reputation to consider. If it gets around that you have . . . behaved badly, it could be a problem for me. People will blame me."

"The way they blamed Dot," said Ida.

"Dot is being blamed for no reason," said

Trudy. "I'd be blamed because you went against my reasonable advice."

"I did say—the way you told me to—something nice to Mr. Langly."

"Good! What did you say?"

"That his dog was nice." Ida paused. "It was the best I could do."

"Oh, Ida!" cried Trudy, but she smiled.

After a few moments of silence, Trudy said, "I'm afraid I have to tell you something else you won't like."

Ida actually groaned. "What?"

"Yesterday as I was leaving school, Mr. Roscoe came up to me. He told me you are doing all right in Latin. But not as well as you could. He doesn't want to give Mr. Langly any reason to expel you. You need to study more."

"How does he know about it all?"

"Remember what I told you when you first came? That small towns have big eyes and ears? Well, schools have big mouths, too. All the teachers know you're my boarder. Everybody knows what Mr. Langly said to you. Believe me, Mr. Langly would be happy to get rid of all the Secret Sisters."

"Would he really do that?"

"It's possible. He once told me it was a mistake to give women the vote. So, Ida, pay attention to Mr. Roscoe. He is trying to help you. A good thing. You're a smart girl and a promising student. All the teachers like you. I urge you to study hard so you can come out on top and show that you are an exemplary student. And by doing well, you'll be a credit to me, too."

"Do I have to be better than everyone else?"

"That's often the way it is for women."

"I'm not a woman!" cried an exasperated Ida.

"You'll be one sooner than you think," returned Trudy.

Ida wondered if that was another warning, but all she said was "My pa says time is the fastest thing in the world."

"I hope you appreciate how smart your parents are."

After dinner, a troubled Ida went up to her room, resolved to study her Latin. Instead, she picked up *Little Women*. *I'll read just a little bit to settle myself.* How would Meg, Jo, Beth, and Amy grow up? How would she, Ida, grow up?

Did she want to know? Of course she did. *Besides*, she told herself, *you can't stop getting older.* It was like a book: to find out what happens, you need to turn the pages. *And every day in my life is like a new page. What did Pa say? "Use what you have, or you'll wind up having nothing."*

So, if I want to know what will happen to the March sisters, I have to keep turning pages. And if I want to know what will happen to me, I have to keep turning my own pages.

With that, Ida sat back in her bed and kept reading.

TWENTY-ONE

On Sunday, Ida took up her pencil and thought about what she would write home. Should she tell them she might be expelled—and all the things that led to that? *No*, she told herself. *They'll only worry.*

> *Dear Everybody,*
>
> *I rode on a train! A locomotive! It was amazing, and scary, and most of all WONDERFUL. I can't wait to tell you about it. Someday I will fly an airplane over our house. And wave. Please wave back!*

The train took me to visit my best friend, Dot, who lives in Oak Creek. I got to know her family.

Here I am, back in Steamboat, only twenty miles away from you, but everything is so different. And people say Denver is even more different. One of my friends—Lulu—has a cousin who lives in New York City. She says it has more than five MILLION people. I don't know if I believe it.

This is considered the modern world. But sometimes people have strange ideas. All mixed up. Like me, sometimes.

You know what? I think the older you get, the more mixed up you get, and then you have to unmix things. It's easier when you are told what to do. The trouble is, I hate being told what to do. To be modern, you have to unmix yourself.

But guess what? I used a telephone! It's the bee's knees!

If we had one, I'd call you every hour.

I love you all! Felix, Ma, Pa, Shelby, Teddy, Snooker, and Bluebell. The sheep. Even the chickens.

Your daughter and sister and once upon a long,
long, long time ago your milkmaid,
Ida Bidson XXXxOOOo
(That means four kisses and four hugs. The little
ones are for Shelby.)

TWENTY-TWO

SEVERAL DAYS PASSED without incident. Then, at the end of one algebra class, Miss Mickle asked Ida to stay behind. "I'd like to talk to you," she said.

Ida exchanged a "what's that about?" look with Dot, who said, "I'll wait in the hall."

As the other students left, Ida remained at her desk.

The teacher was smiling. "How are things going?" she said.

"Fine, thank you."

"Have you heard any more from Mr. Langly?"

"No. Have you?"

Instead of answering, Miss Mickle said, "Ida, ever since we first met, when you were registering—remember that silly mix-up?—I've been paying attention to you. So, I just wanted to let you know, you're doing fine in algebra, but you could do much better. You're smart enough to be the best in class. And being the best might be a good thing."

"Why?"

"It will make it harder for Mr. Langly to expel you."

Ida sighed. "That's what Miss Sedgewick told me."

"That's the way it sometimes is."

"For modern girls?"

Miss Mickle grimaced. "For modern girls."

"Miss Mickle," said Ida, "I think you're the best teacher."

"Among us modern girls?" said Miss Mickle with a laugh.

Ida, grinning, nodded.

"Thank you. That means a lot to me." Miss Mickle offered a warm smile. "Just know I'm here to help."

"What was that?" asked Dot as Ida came out of the classroom.

"I need to study more. Miss Mickle said if I get really good grades, it would be harder for Mr. Langly to expel me. Trudy told me the same thing."

"Least you're doing okay. I'm not doing so great in science."

"Want me to help you?"

"Could you?"

"I was a teacher, remember? I'll ask if you can come over to Trudy's house after school tomorrow. Ask your mom if you can stay over."

"Copacetic."

That evening, at dinner, Ida asked Trudy if Dot could come over for help in science.

"What about your own studies?"

"At school in Elk Valley, being a teacher meant I learned more."

"Tomorrow I have to go to Hayden," said Trudy. "I don't know when I'll be back. I'm not sure it's a good idea; I don't really know anything about her. But I suppose she can come. Only Ida, please, promise, *nothing* wild."

"I know. Can she stay over?"

"I'll have to think about that."

"She's my best friend. I want so much to help her."

"I'll need to speak to her mother," Trudy said.

"Her phone number is one-two-four-six."

"Why don't you call?"

"You'll have to show me how."

Ida called, and it was arranged.

The following day, Dot walked to Trudy's house with Ida after school. They settled in the living room and had just gotten out their science textbooks when there was a knock on the door.

Ida opened it. Helene was standing there. "Dot told me you're studying here. I could use some math help."

Ida let her in.

Twenty minutes later, both Becky and Lulu came to the door.

"Can we study with you?" asked Lulu.

"We have to organize this," said Ida. "Who's good at what? We'll help each other."

It didn't take long for the girls to divide up. Those who were good in one subject worked with someone who was not so good. Then they switched around so everybody got the help they needed.

"Are you bad at anything?" Lulu asked Ida.

"Not so great in Latin," Ida admitted.

"I'm good," said Lulu. "I don't know why."

"Because you speak Flapper," said Helene.

Laughter.

"Everybody," Ida called out, "guess what? Miss Sedgewick told me Mr. Langly would like to get rid of all of us."

"Why?" asked Helene.

"We're too modern. But do you know what I think? If we are really good students, we can show him up."

"We should meet every afternoon," Becky said.

"Here?" asked Ida.

"Can we?" said Helene. "We've got just two weeks till exams."

"I'll ask Trudy."

"This is going to be the monkey's uncle," said Helene.

"Better than that," said Lulu.

"What?"

"Modern pie in Mr. Langly's face," said Lulu.

Laughter.

"You know what my pa is always saying?" Ida said: "'Work, not wishes, whips the job.'"

They were still working when Trudy came home. "My goodness," she exclaimed, not looking pleased. "Is this a secret party?"

"We're studying," said Ida. "Everybody, this is Miss Sedgewick. This is her house. This is Dot, Lulu, Helene, and Becky, and me. The Secret Sisters. We're going to show Mr. Langly what we can do by studying together and getting the best grades."

"And we promise," Lulu called out, "not to dance."

Everybody's eyes were on Trudy as she stood still for a moment. Then she smiled. "I guess," she said, "I can be modern too. I used to be a teacher. Like Ida. Who needs help?"

Dot and Lulu raised their hands.

From then on, every day after school, the Secret Sisters got together at Trudy's house to coach, quiz, and teach one another. When Trudy returned from work, she tutored the girls. At night she made cookies. Cake. And lemonade.

There was much work. Reviews. Memory tasks. Quizzes. There was also laughter. But everyone knew they were running out of time.

One evening, when Ida and Trudy were having dinner, Trudy said, "Your friend Dot is really quite smart. And do you know, I rather like Lulu."

"She's the monkey's necktie."

Trudy laughed. "I think that describes her

exactly." Then she added, "Ida, I admit, your friends are hard workers."

"Do you know what Lulu called you?"

"Do I want to know?"

"Said you were a pearl."

Trudy put a hand to her heart. "Thank you," she said quietly.

Ida saw her eyes glisten.

TWENTY-THREE

THE SECRET SISTERS were having their regular lunch together when Lulu rushed in. "Miss Mickle was fired!"

"How do you know?" Helene demanded.

"Just met her in the hallway, and she told me."

"Did she say why?" asked Ida.

"Said it's about that time she taught us the Charleston and because she played loud, jazzy music in her classes. Some parents complained to Mr. Langly. So, he fired her. Just waited till he could find a replacement. She'll be gone this week."

"He's probably got some dumb Dora to replace her," said Becky.

"Langly is mean," said Dot.

"His dog would be a better principal," said Lulu bitterly.

"Is she really going right away?" asked Ida.

"Said she's catching the Thursday train to Denver," said Lulu. "Oh, but she's going to give us—our club—her phonograph machine, if we want it. Said she can't take it with her. But she hopes we keep dancing."

Absorbing the news, the girls sat silently.

"She's such a good teacher," said Ida.

"I agree," said Becky.

"Everybody who has her loves her," said Helene. "Can we do anything to keep her?"

"Talk to Mr. Langly," said Becky.

"He won't listen," said Lulu. "He's such a Father Time."

"But we have to do *something*," said Dot. "It's a bit our fault. Isn't it?" She glanced at Lulu. "We're the ones who asked her to teach us the Charleston."

"But she was playing that music in her classes before then," Lulu pointed out.

"And our meeting took place *after* school," added Becky.

"I don't think Langly will listen," said Ida.

"But he's making a mistake," said Helene.

Ida said, "Trudy says he really wants the school to be the best, then he goes and fires one of the best teachers. He thinks getting rid of her will stop us from dancing—and stop everything else he thinks is modern! We have to do something."

"If we do say something to him," Dot added slowly, "and Miss Mickle hears about it, it might make her feel better, knowing we are still on her side."

"When would we do it?" said Helene.

"She's going this week, so it has to be right away," said Lulu. "This afternoon. After last class. We'll all do it. Agreed?"

For a moment no one spoke.

"Better not tell Miss Mickle what we're going to do," said Helene. "She might tell us not to."

Ida shook her head. "I don't think I should be the one to tell Langly."

"Why not?" asked Becky.

"Langly said if I do one more bad thing, he'll expel me."

"But this isn't bad," said Helene.

"He'll think it is," said Ida.

"Miss Mickle is your favorite teacher," said Helene. "And you're her pet. And the only one still with pigtails."

"And the shortest," said Becky.

"And," said Lulu, "you're the bravest."

"But . . . he'll expel me."

For a moment no one spoke.

"Then," said Lulu, "I should be the one to speak to him."

"You?" cried Ida with surprise. "Why?"

"I suggested the dancing. And guess what? I don't mind telling Langly what I think of him. He's doing something wrong. And what's the point of being a flapper if you don't say what you think?"

"But . . . but what if he kicks you out?" asked Ida.

"Guess what?"

"What?"

"I won't go."

For a moment no one spoke.

Lulu said, "Lots of kids have been kicked out of school. I'll be the first one to kick *in*. I'll have a dance party right here every Saturday."

Applause.

It was Ida who said, "Lulu, you really are the cat's pajamas."

Louder applause.

Helene said, "Agreed. We will go to Langly right after school."

As Ida and Dot walked to study hall, Ida said, "I'm almost looking forward to meeting with Langly. Just to hear what Lulu will say. Only thing is, when Trudy hears about all this, she could be the one to send me away."

"No, she won't," said Dot. "She really loves you."

Ida looked at Dot.

"She told me. She really did. That you were one of the best things ever to happen to her. And guess what?"

"What?"

"Everybody loves you."

"Not Mr. Langly."

"True."

Right after the last class, the Secret Sisters walked into Mr. Langly's office. Miss Ogden was seated at her desk. She looked up from her work. "Yes, girls? Is something the matter?"

Lulu said, "We would like to speak to Mr. Langly."

"All of you?"

"All," said Lulu.

"What would it be about?"

"He's fired Miss Mickle—" Ida started.

Lulu finished the sentence. "And we want to tell him that he shouldn't."

"I see . . ." said Miss Ogden. She looked doubtful.

"We have to see him," said Becky.

Miss Ogden considered and then stood up. "I'll see if he's free," she said, and went into the inner office.

"Think he'll even listen to us?" asked Dot.

"He's one mealy potato," said Lulu.

The door opened and Miss Ogden reappeared. Right behind her was Mr. Langly, looking stern. He was polishing his glasses. By his side was his dog, wagging his tail.

"Yes, girls? Miss Ogden tells me you wish to see me. I only have a few seconds."

Lulu stepped forward. "It's about Miss Mickle. We know she's been fired, but we wanted to say we really, really like her. Everybody does. Just because she plays music people like is no reason to get rid of her."

Momentarily, Ida closed her eyes. Her heart was pounding. She could not restrain herself. She blurted out, "And she's a great teacher. If you want to have a great school, you shouldn't fire great teachers."

"Well, yes," said Mr. Langly. "She is going. I had to make the decision as to what's best for our students."

"But if she's so good, why are you dumping her?" called out Helene.

Mr. Langly put his glasses back on. "Principals make decisions in the best interest of students. Need I add, you are all too young to make such judgments.

"And I should remind all of you that preliminary term grades will be given out soon, and you'll want to be sure you have passed. May I recall the proverb 'No one is so poor as an ignorant person.'"

Ida cried out, "It's an ignorant person who makes foolish judgments."

Mr. Langly drew himself up. "I have important work to do. Principals are busy people. You are no more than children. Good afternoon."

With that, Mr. Langly took his dog back into his office. The door slammed behind them.

"Sorry," said Miss Ogden. "I liked her too."

The girls went out into the hall. "What a kill-joy," said Becky.

"Absolutely low lid," agreed Dot.

"Total nowhere," said Helene.

"Canceled stamp," added Lulu.

"We need to show Miss Mickle—and every-one—we're on her side, and that we won't stop being modern," said Ida. "I have an idea. Only, it is a bit wild."

"What is it?" said Becky.

Ida shared her idea.

"The real McCoy," said Lulu.

On Thursday at five o'clock, there were already people at the train depot, ready to board the 5:20 to Denver. Among them were the Secret Sisters, standing around Miss Mickle's phonograph machine. Lulu had wound it up, and a record was on the turntable.

Becky, who was posted to keep watch, cried out, "Here she comes!"

Miss Mickle, in coat and cloche hat, carrying

a suitcase, was quickly approaching the station.

Ida began to snap her fingers. That was when Lulu flicked the switch on the phonograph and set the needle on the record. "The Charleston," played by the Hoosier Radio Boys, blared out. With that, the girls began to dance, each enthusiastically doing her own kicking, hand-waving, arm-flapping variation.

Miss Mickle stopped, looked, and laughed. Then she came forward, dropped her suitcase, flung off her coat, and joined in the dancing. Some of the waiting passengers smiled and applauded. A few waved their arms as if joining in too. There were no frowns.

A whistle screeched, announcing the train's arrival.

"One more time," urged Miss Mickle, resetting the needle on the record. As the girls continued to dance, the teacher gave each of them a hug. Then she grabbed her suitcase and coat and rushed onto the train. The Sisters were still dancing when it pulled out, the loud whistle blending in with the music, Miss Mickle at a window, waving, laughing.

"Least she knows we liked her music," said

Dot when the train had gone.

"And her dance," said Lulu.

"And her," said Ida.

That evening, Ida sat with Trudy in the kitchen, eating dinner.

Ida said, "Do you know about Miss Mickle?"

"I'm afraid so. And I heard about the send-off your Secret Sisters gave her. I suspect the whole town knows."

"What are people saying?"

"Apparently, they loved it. Miss Mickle had made more friends here than I realized, and it seems your gesture was appreciated."

"Miss Mickle was fired because of that music she played," said Ida. "What was so bad about it? If being wild is what she is, I'm going to be wild." She waited for Trudy's criticism.

"I've gotten to know your friends," said Trudy. "And I do like them. They are good girls. I'm sure Miss Mickle was touched by your send-off. I wish her well. But Ida, the music was *not* the only reason she was let go."

"What do you mean?"

After a moment of quiet, Trudy said, "It seems

that when Miss Mickle took the teacher position here, she neglected to inform Mr. Langly that she was married."

"Married!"

"Apparently her husband is also a teacher—in Denver. She couldn't get a position there, so she came up here—her first job—to gain experience."

"I love the way she teaches," said Ida.

"As I once told you, Mr. Langly doesn't believe a woman can be married and be a good teacher."

"Is he married?"

"Yes."

"Are the men teachers at school married?"

"Yes."

"Then it's not fair, and Mr. Langly is a four-flusher!"

"Now, Ida . . ."

"Does that mean if I become a teacher, I can't get married?"

"I'm afraid women have to make hard choices."

"You didn't choose," Ida blurted out.

"What . . . what do you mean?"

"The man you were going to marry died."

Trudy's face filled with pain. She became silent.

Ida, realizing she had hurt Trudy badly, stammered, "I'm . . . I'm sorry. I . . . I didn't mean that. That was awful to say."

Trudy bowed her head for a full minute. Then she looked up. "I accept your apology," she said, her voice strained. "But you mustn't tell any of your friends what I've told you about Miss Mickle. It's a private matter."

"If Miss Mickle told the truth about being married," said Ida, trying to think it through, "she wouldn't have gotten the job. Is *that* fair?"

"But Ida, telling a lie can't be right, can it?"

"Maybe she really needed a job, and telling the lie was the only way she could get one."

Trudy sighed. "In the adult world, that can happen."

"Then the adult world is stupid!" cried Ida. "The Secret Sisters will do things better."

"I hope so," said Trudy.

Neither spoke until Trudy moved to change the subject. "Now, how are your classes going?"

"Fine. Trudy, I had to do something about Miss Mickle. I hate doing nothing."

"As it happened, I saw Mr. Langly today. Ida, he's not truly a bad man. He loves the school. Wants to make it the best. But he's old-fashioned.

He did let me know he's still considering expelling you. I'm sure he knows about your dance down by the railroad. I'm afraid you've been caught up a bit too much with your new friends."

"I love them!" cried Ida.

"Ida, if you don't come back to school in November, you won't be able to see them."

That silenced Ida.

"I urge you to study, study, study. Make it impossible for Langly to ask you to leave."

"Will that work?"

"I hope so. I'd miss you a great deal."

"Thank you," said Ida through tears. "I really want to stay. Here."

"We shall have to see," said Trudy.

"Can I say something?"

"Of course."

"You're very kind."

"And can I say something?" said Trudy.

Ida nodded.

"I love your being here. It fills me with hope."

Ida said, "'Hope is the thing with feathers.'"

To which Trudy replied, "We must never stop flying."

TWENTY-FOUR

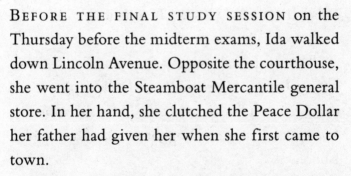

BEFORE THE FINAL STUDY SESSION on the Thursday before the midterm exams, Ida walked down Lincoln Avenue. Opposite the courthouse, she went into the Steamboat Mercantile general store. In her hand, she clutched the Peace Dollar her father had given her when she first came to town.

"How can I help you?" the saleslady asked Ida when she approached a counter.

"I want a necklace that has lots of parts."

"What do you mean, parts?"

"I need to give people the bits. My special friends."

"How much money do you have?"

Ida held up her Peace Dollar.

"Some people save those. Are you sure you want to spend it?"

Ida nodded.

The lady was thoughtful for a few moments. Then she said, "I may have just the right thing for you."

She led the way to a small jewelry counter and got out a bracelet, which she draped over her hand. A half dozen white beads were strung on a golden cord. "Now, these, just so you know, are not true pearls. But they are good imitation ones. What they call 'D luster.' Indestructible."

"How much does it cost?"

"A real special. Ninety-five cents."

Ida handed over the Peace Dollar and put the pearl bracelet in her pocket. Then she took the five cents change and bought a yard of bright blue ribbon.

Once home, Ida took the bracelet apart, joined the study session in the living room, and then went on with her own studies late into the night.

The next day, Friday, everyone took their exams.

After school, despite the chill, the Secret

Sisters gathered out on the front lawn. What would happen next?

No one knew.

From her pocket, Ida took out her handful of pearls. "Just in case we never meet again, I have something for you all." She gave each Secret Sister one pearl. "They aren't real. But my love for each of you is," she announced.

There were hugs. There were tears. Promises to stay in touch.

"Good luck!

"Do well!"

"No failing allowed!"

For dinner that night, Trudy served beef stew with dumplings. "I hope this is not our last meal together," she said. "Do you like it?"

"Copacetic!"

"Oh, Ida, I do hope your grades are so strong Langly can't ask you to leave," said Trudy. "I'd miss you so much if you didn't come back."

"I'd miss you too," said Ida. "Did you speak to Mr. Langly again?"

"I told him you were good for the school, and that it would be a grave mistake to expel you."

"What did he say?"

"Nothing. That's like him."

"I don't like him."

Trudy leaned forward and whispered, "I don't either."

Ida grinned.

Trudy reached out and squeezed Ida's hand. Ida squeezed back.

That night Ida pulled Pa's old suitcase out from under the bed and opened it. Into it she put the *We love you!* note signed by her family.

Just to look at it made Ida's heart swell.

She went and stood before the mirror and used her new ribbon to tie off her braids. She was glad she had kept them. *I'm a high school girl*, she told herself, *with wonderful friends. Oh, I do want to go home, but I so want to come back, too!*

She packed up her clothing.

The next morning at about eleven—it was Saturday—Ida knew Pa had arrived when she heard the series of backfires from the old car.

She rushed out to meet him and flung her arms around him.

"She's been a wonderful guest," Trudy told Mr. Bidson.

Then Ida turned to Trudy. "I have something for you. A thank-you present."

"Ida, you shouldn't have."

Ida held out a pearl, and when Trudy, speechless, took it, Ida asked, "May I hug you?" She wrapped her arms around Trudy and squeezed hard. As she did, she said, "You're a Secret Sister too."

"Bless you."

To keep out the chill, Pa had brought a sheep's fleece to wrap around Ida as they drove home.

"Well, how was it?" he asked once they got going.

"Copacetic," said Ida grimly.

"Which means?"

"Good."

"Do well enough to go back?"

"Hope. What if I don't?"

"I guess you can stay home."

"Pa, if I'm going to be a teacher, I can't stay home."

Pa nodded. "Understood."

In her head, she said a prayer. *Please, please, just please let me come back.*

TWENTY-FIVE

THERE WAS SNOW on the side of the driveway
up to the log cabin. The moment the car stopped,
Felix came rushing forward and all but knocked
Ida over with his hug. Ma appeared with baby
Shelby—who offered Ida a real smile—in her
arms. Teddy, the sheepdog, barked and wagged
his tail furiously.

"Look at you," cried Ma. "Everyone is so
happy to see you."

Oh, it was good to be home! Everything as it
should be. Everything familiar. Everything sweet.
Everything cozy. Everything loving. Everything
right. How good that nothing had changed, even

as Ida knew *she* had changed and had learned so much and lived in a bigger world. It amazed her that her family didn't seem to notice.

Before dinner, Ida sat on a stool and milked Bluebell the way she used to do. "Did you miss me?" she asked.

When Bluebell swatted her with her mucky tail, Ida buried her face into the cow's side and drew a deep breath. Bluebell smelled wonderful. "I do love your smell," she said. "But I don't want to be a milkmaid."

That evening, Ida found time to be alone with her mother. She told her all about Trudy, Dot, Lulu, Becky, Helene, and Miss Mickle, and how different they were. "Do you know what I want?"

Ma shook her head.

"I want to be like all of them but be myself, too. I want to be smart, careful, sincere, full of fun, and experience lots and lots of new things all the time. Be the most modern girl in the world. Is that impossible?"

"If anyone can do it, you can."

"Oh, Ma, I'm so glad to be home. I love it here. I love you. And Pa. And Felix and Shelby. Everybody. But I love my new friends, too. Is it wrong for me to want to go back so badly?"

"Honey, it seems to me that when you start sharing your love outside your home, it means you're growing up. When I was young, I thought nothing would change. And then . . . everything did."

"I want to change," said Ida, feeling her eyes fill with tears. "But you have to promise *you* won't change."

Ma smiled. "All children want their parents not to change. But guess what? We do too. I want to show you something."

She led Ida to a box sitting on a shelf. "Look what I saved," she said.

"My letters," said Ida, with a questioning look at Ma.

"With room for lots more," said Ma.

"Oh, Ma," cried Ida, "no matter what I do, I'll always write. I will! And I'll never stop loving you."

"Just make sure you fill your letters with adventures."

Ida hugged her ma as tightly as she ever had. It was only then that she realized she had grown taller.

★ ★ ★

Every day, Ida walked the mile to their mailbox. On the fifth day, the letter she was waiting for came.

> *This is to affirm that Ida Bidson passed all her exams with high honors and will be welcomed back for the remainder of the term.*
>
> *Mr. Langly*
> *Principal*

At the dinner table, Ida held up the letter. "High honors," she announced. "I'm going back to school."

There was a moment of silence, and then Felix said, "My sister is the smartest girl in the world!"

Ida laughed and cried at the same time.

Two days later there was another letter. It was from Trudy.

> *My dear Ida,*
> *I am <u>so</u> happy you are coming back. And when you do, there will be a big change. I've spoken to Mrs. Kovács and suggested that Dot come and*

live with us. I think she will. I do have that extra
room. I'll have a house full of young sisters.
    Sincerely,
    Trudy

On the Monday morning when the term resumed, Ida and Dot had breakfast together with Trudy. Ida couldn't stop smiling at the sight of Dot at Trudy's table, and she had never seen her friend happier than she had been the day before, when she'd arrived carrying her small suitcase. Excited, they kept talking about Lulu, Helene, and Becky, wondering if they would be back in school, too.

"I'm sure they will," said Trudy.

"Do you know for certain?" asked Dot.

"No, but it would be such a good thing. That's why I'm sure of it. Now, off you go. Go meet your Secret Sisters."

Ida and Dot needed no further prompting. Within five minutes, they were out the door, all but running toward school. They barely got halfway down the first street when Ida abruptly halted. "Forgot my Latin book. Wait here. Be right back."

She raced to the house and went in, but as she

started to pass the living room, she saw Trudy
standing in front of Ralph Warren's photograph.
Trudy was so focused on the photo, her face a
mix of sadness and joy, that Ida paused.

"We finally have a family," Trudy was saying
to the picture.

Quietly, Ida backed out of the house and hurried to catch up with Dot.

"Get it?" Dot called.

"Couldn't find it. I'll use yours," Ida replied,
and they rushed on.

Ida and Dot were the first ones at the school.
Then Helene showed up, followed by Becky.

"Has anyone seen Lulu?" asked Helene.

"Here I am!" cried Lulu as she ran up. "Guess
what? Miss Gemelli gave my old man the mitt
and handcuffed the pastor instead. Hot diggity
dog!"

Applause.

"The Secret Sisters are back together!" exclaimed Ida.

More applause, and hugs all around.

Ida began to snap her fingers, and when the
school doors opened, the girls linked their arms
and marched forward, singing in their sweet,
clear voices:

"Ain't we got fun?
Not much money, oh, but honey
Ain't we got fun?
The rent's unpaid, dear
We haven't a car
But in any way, dear
We'll stay as we are
Even if we owe the grocer
Don't we have fun?
Tax collector's getting closer
Still, we have fun!
There's nothing surer
The rich get rich, and the poor get poorer
In the meantime, in between time
Ain't we got fun?"

And as they sang, the Secret Sisters swept into
school.

Author's Note

WHAT MADE THE 1920S SPECIAL?

The United States had recently fought in World War I (1914–1918), during which some 117,000 American soldiers died. An additional 675,000 Americans died in the 1918–1920 flu epidemic. In short, the years leading up to the start of the decade had been a time of suffering and grief for countless people. Those who escaped the misery of war and sickness must have felt an immense sense of relief, and many were ready to put the memory of these rough years behind them.

It was also a time of great political change. By the end of the war in Europe, the Russian, German, Austro-Hungarian, and Turkish empires had ceased to be, and the United States of America had emerged as an important world power.

Radical ideas of all kinds—left and right—were common and spreading.

Simultaneously, American social life was changing. The number of people living on farms and ranches decreased. The number of city dwellers increased. There were more and more factories. The common use of the automobile went way up. In 1920, women were allowed to vote for the first time, and young women in particular were liberated in terms of dress, speech, and social rules, giving rise to flapper culture.

The telephone, radio, and movies became part of everyday life for those who could make use of and afford them. It was also during this period that obtaining a high school education became increasingly standard.

That said, religious bigotry, racial discrimination, and anti-immigration laws and attitudes hardened. Prohibition—making alcoholic drinks illegal—came into force in 1920. Organized crime increased. So did the power of the racist Ku Klux Klan.

All and all, it was a complicated and rapidly changing era.

Steamboat Springs, Colorado, is a real place. It got its name—so the tale goes—when white explorers went into the area, heard the noise of spurting hot springs, and thought it sounded like steamboats.

The high school Ida attends in the story still stands and functions as a school, but the names I used for the school's faculty and students are fictional.

You can turn to YouTube to explore a number of things in this book: You can watch the original 1924 silent film *The Thief of Bagdad*. You can listen to a number of renditions of "Ain't We Got Fun?" You can even watch lessons on dancing the Charleston.

Little Women, the two-part novel by Louisa May Alcott (1832–1888), was published in 1868 and 1869 and was the most popular book among young women readers well into the twentieth century. It is still read widely, and several movie versions have been made, including one in 2019. You can watch a number of these films on You-Tube, or, like Ida, you can check out a copy of the book from your local library and read it for yourself.

Glossary of 1920s Flapper Slang

ab-so-lute-ly: favorable
airtight: perfect
apple sauce: flattery
babes: women
bee's knees: an extraordinary person, thing, or idea
best berries: very appealing
bobbed: hair cut short
bubblehead: vapid or foolish person
bum's rush: to eject a person from a place
butter-and-egg man: the man with the money
buzz: great idea
cat's pajamas: new and cool, wonderful
chassis: the female body
copacetic: wonderful, agreeable, fine
creepers: unpleasant
cutting a rug: dancing

dodo: a simpleton

duck's quack: excellent, splendid

ducky: very good

dumb Dora: a foolish woman

fakeloo artist: a con man, a phony

Father Time: any man over thirty

fish fingers: great

flapper: modern, stylish young woman with short hair who wears short skirts

flat tire: a boring pest

Get a wiggle on: Hurry up!

giggle water: an alcoholic beverage

gink: a foolish person, one who is socially inept

goofy: in love, crazy

handcuffed: to be engaged to marry

heebie-jeebies: extreme anxiety, jitters

hip: informed, aware

hoofer: a chorus girl/dancer

Hot diggity dog: Wow!

hot dog: how great

icy mitt: being rejected

Jane: any woman

Jeepers creepers: Wow!

jingle-brained: not very smart

kick the can: to put off till later

killjoy: a person who takes the fun out of things

kippy: good, nice
live wire: an energetic person
low lid: not classy
lucky pup: a fortunate person
Lulu: a gangster's sweetheart
mealy potato: not worth anything
the mitt: the wrong side of the hand, a slap, rejection
monkey's necktie/monkey's uncle: a unique person
nerts: nonsense
nifty: great, excellent
oil can: unique
old fogies: old-fashioned people
old man: father
peep: see
peppy: energetic
piffle pill: nonsense
prune pit: old-fashioned
the real McCoy: authentic
ripe rube: a bumpkin, a sucker
sinker: a bad idea
snail's elbows: something unusual
snuggle pup's bow-how: terrific
spill you later: chat at another time
splosh: a dull or drab person

sucking balloons: wasting time
swanky: classy, ritzy
sweet cookie: a person who is nice
swell thing: fine, excellent
take the air: go away
tiger's spots: see *cat's pajamas*
tight: perfect
total nowhere: someone who knows nothing
wurp: a dull person
zoom: energy

About the Author

Avi is the multi-award-winning author of more than eighty books for children. He received Newbery Honors for *The True Confessions of Charlotte Doyle* and *Nothing but the Truth: A Documentary Novel* and the Newbery Medal for *Crispin: The Cross of Lead*. His many other popular novels include *Poppy*, *The Fighting Ground*, *Loyalty*, and *The Good Dog*, as well as Ida Bidson's first adventure, *The Secret School*, winner of the California Young Reader Medal.

Avi lives in the Colorado mountains, not far from the school Ida would have attended.

AVI-WRITER.COM